Truth to Tell:
Stories from
Here and Away

by

Allison Mitcham

DREAMCATCHER PUBLISHING
Saint John • New Brunswick • Canada

DreamCatcher Publishing acknowledges the support of the New Brunswick Arts Council.

Canadian Cataloguing in Publication Data

Mitcham, Allison - 1932

Truth to Tell: Stories from Here and Away

ISBN - 1-894372-30-1
    I. Title.
PS8576.I86T78 2004   C813'.54   C2004-902849-9

Editor: Yvonne Wilson

Typesetter: Chas Goguen

Cover Design: Dawn Drew, INK Graphic Design Services Corp.

Printed and bound in Canada

DREAMCATCHER PUBLISHING INC.
105 Prince William Street
Saint John, New Brunswick, Canada E2L 2B2
www.dreamcatcherbooks.ca

"If circumstances lead me, I will find
Where truth is hid, though it were hid indeed
Within the centre."

- Hamlet

TABLE OF CONTENTS

FOREWORD

The stories in this book are fiction, although the first person narration might lead the reader to assume that the characters are dead ringers for people I have known. I trust that this disclaimer, however, makes the people, circumstances and settings in this book none the less 'real'. I am inclined to agree with Gabrielle Roy's somewhat paradoxical contention that the best way to get at the elusive truth about people and situations is *not* through an exact factual recounting, but a fictional rendition.

I wish to thank my family for their continuing interest in my writing - in this instance, particularly my daughters, Stephanie and Naomi, the first to read these stories and encourage me to go on with them; my good friend, Dr. Theresia Quigley, author and Professor of English and Comparative Literature, for once more enthusiastically endorsing my work; my editor, Yvonne Wilson, and publisher, Elizabeth Margaris at DreamCatcher Publishing for their loyalty, support and friendship.

- Allison Mitcham
June 2004

NEVER KID A KIDDER

From Miscou in northern New Brunswick to Pictou, Nova Scotia, travellers on roads bordering the Gulf of Saint Lawrence and the Northumberland Strait have, now and then over the years, reported seeing a burning ship far out on the water, and, sometimes, at about the same time, an ethereal presence, a woman in white, on the nearby shore. Although, according to all accounts, the ship is old-fashioned, a schooner, its sails and masts aflame, some of the travellers observing these sights have been contemporary. Several are seemingly credible witnesses from practical walks of life - among them a doctor, a mechanic and a nurse - who attest, moreover, to having been stone cold sober when they noticed these strange apparitions, as well as being generally disinclined to believe in supernatural manifestations.

One of the infrequently discussed appearances of this burning vessel was supposed to have been off the Strait island where we now live, although this recorded sighting was not recent but, as far as I can make out, dates back about ninety years. My mother told me the story when I was a child growing up on the mainland across from the island. She said she had heard it from her mother. Since my mother was a world-class teller of tales, most of them about giants and other fantastic beings caught up in magical situations, I automatically relegated the burning ship and the woman in white to the part of my mind inhabited by imaginary events and beings.

Although other mainlanders besides my mother sometimes mention the burning ship and the woman in white, the islanders do not. Nor do our island friends ever comment on the sea serpent which the islander-turned-mainlander, who sold us this farm, assured us lived not so long ago in the pond at the bottom of our newly-acquired property. Perhaps they find such seemingly outlandish tales unworthy of their attention, or maybe their reluctance to discuss these topics is because they fear ridicule from relative newcomers like ourselves. It could be simply their natural Scottish reserve.

The old people are not a garrulous lot, and since we have only lived here for twenty years, whereas they and their forebears have been rooted on this island for more than two hundred, we hesitate to ask questions which they might find impertinent. On a small island like this, seven miles from the mainland, you daren't risk being even marginally at odds with anyone: we all depend too much on one another. Besides, since these firmly-entrenched neighbors of ours have always treated us with great kindness and generosity, we do not want to overstep any boundaries by offending them.

Not so Uncle Archie, my mother's half brother. Much younger than she and without responsibilities, he has few, if any, inhibitions. I have often, as far back as I can remember, heard my mother say in exasperation, "Archie will march in where angels fear to tread."

When I was growing up, Archie used to appear without warning at my parents' house - mostly at mealtimes. Now, on the island, during the fishing season, he materializes in the same way at our back door before supper, giving himself just time for a beer or two before we eat. I hear he drops in on a few of the islanders as well, mostly in the early evening. He claims to be distantly related to some of them. Apparently, they give him tea and feed him too.

Although Archie doesn't fish any more, he still spends the fishing season in a shanty at the island's east end, a decaying structure he laid claim to years ago. There, amidst the colony of active fishermen, living in slightly more up-at-the-heels huts within sight of their anchored boats, Archie appears to thrive on the all-male camaraderie. I figure the fishermen tolerate him because they think he is a card, a would-be comedian who never seems to run out of funny stories.

It's hard to tell which are basically true and which are mostly fictional. He manages to make all of them sound convincing. I've always thought Archie's stories grow from a seed of truth and that his fertile imagination embellishes them magnificently. But this is just conjecture. Archie will never give a straightforward answer about their origins - or anything else for that matter. He's always kidding around, so you don't know what's what. Sometimes I find this quality of his exasperating. I suppose I'm not the only one.

Archie and a handful of the other transients get around the island on four-wheelers they've brought over from the mainland. From time to time during the two months they are resident here, they zoom up and down the four miles of dirt road, dusting the alders and lowbush cranberries as well as a few dogs and children.

Mostly the sparse traffic stops at nightfall, and deep quiet ensues. Only, by times, do the waves breaking on the shore, the wind in the poplars and the coyotes howling out their eerie messages to one another break into this silence. The old people tend to go to bed early, except on rare evenings when there's a card party: the fishermen have to retire soon after supper because every weekday they are up at three-thirty or four and out on the water by five - unless, of course, it's so stormy that they can't risk going out to their traps.

If, midweek, we do hear a vehicle on the road late at night or in the wee hours of the morning, we assume it's Archie and wonder sleepily where he is going - or coming from. Since there is no store, no restaurant, no bar, not even any streetlights because there is no electricity on the island, we are hard-pressed to guess what would lure him out when everyone else is comatose. We assume he is in motion out there because he is bored and still feeling lively, and leave it at that. He doesn't have to get up early, and, apart from cutting a bit of wood for his stove, he doesn't work or, it would seem, worry - so he isn't tired.

* * *

It was during one of these late night/early morning forays that Archie claimed he saw the burning ship and the woman in white. In tones of high excitement, he told everyone on the island - everyone who would listen - about his extraordinary experience. I think we were about the last to hear the narrative directly from the horse's mouth, so to speak, though we had had inklings on the wharf and over supper at our good friend Lily's place that Archie had been telling a taller-than-usual tale.

It was Lily who finally sounded us out - in her own hesitant but nonetheless determined fashion. Although we have spent a lot of time with her and love her dearly, she still finds us hard to talk to when the conversation gets much beyond scones and tea, how the grandchildren are keeping, and whose boat she's just seen from her kitchen window. Bringing up an unusual or possibly controversial topic visibly stresses her. When she is driven to make this effort, she metes out her words as reluctantly as a miser his money. I think this is because for most of her adult life she was under her husband's and brothers' thumbs, and, although they are long since dead, she still seems to be waiting for someone else to take control. Jack, my husband, is usually good at doing this. He loves to talk and he can generally put people who are not talkative by nature at their ease. In this instance, though, Lily was obliged to make not only the first move but several subsequent ones.

"So," she began tentatively, "Archie was down to the wharf late last night, wasn't he?" She stopped dead, waiting it would seem, for one of us to take over.

We simply nodded, encouragingly I thought. We weren't exactly sure what she was driving at.

"So we hear," Jack said finally to break the silence.

Then Lily changed tack and asked, "Did you see any light offshore last night?"

"No," we chorused.

"Why?" I asked, and then added, "But we wouldn't have seen anything: we were sound asleep all night."

Then Jack, attempting to be helpful and sounding instead rather foolish to my ears - and, I think, his own - said, "Why would anyone be out on the water last night? ... It's not herring season." He needed more clues from Lily before continuing.

But Lily didn't say anything more about Archie or the strange light just then. Instead, she got up, refilled our teacups slowly and brought out the cookie tin. Then she lit the oil lamp on the kitchen table, although we still had daylight enough to see by.

When she couldn't think of anything else to do, Lily sat down again, took a deep breath and, head lowered as if she were reading a text inscribed on the tabletop, related her story haltingly, like a shy student in her first year at school.

"Archie came by here this morning," she began. "He told me he'd seen a stranger on the road last night - a lady dressed all in white, wet and shivering, standing there, looking like she was waiting for a lift. Well, that's what Archie said he thought she wanted.

"So he pulled up alongside her, stopped his bike and asked her what the trouble was and where she wanted to go. He said she didn't answer, didn't seem to understand.

"Maybe she didn't speak English," he said.

"Then Archie told me that that lady just pointed out to the Strait, way beyond the wharf. When he looked out he said he saw a boat burning - a sailing boat, so far gone that he and this woman stood there together on the road and watched it sink."

Lily looked up at us briefly and then went on doggedly. She was no more ready to stop than she had been to begin. She proceeded with an intensity of concentration I had never seen in her before - except when she was baking.

"Well, Archie said he figured the lady in white must've come from the boat, that she'd floated in or something, which was why she was wet. Archie said he reckoned he'd better take her somewhere and see that she got a hot cup of tea and a change of clothes. But, as everyone else was asleep, he thought he'd have to bring her back to his place.

"So Archie said he patted the buddy seat on the bike to let this strange, silent woman know that she was supposed to ride up there behind him.

"But," says Archie, "before I knew what was what, she was perched there sidesaddle. It was almost like she'd floated up there.

"Well," Archie goes on, "I never did get her down home. Halfway there, just by the cemetery entrance, I feel this cold hand on my arm and nearly run the bike into the ditch. As it was, I stalled the motor, and that lady floated clear of the bike and disappeared down the cemetery road - with a sort of light about her, like an outsized firefly."

Lily looked up expectantly, triumphant too, now that she had completed the task she had set herself. She turned from Jack to me.

"Well, I'll be darned," Jack said, at a loss for words for once. Then he added, grinning, "Archie sure has outdone himself this time."

That was when I realized that Jack, having grown up on the Fundy shore, hadn't ever heard the old story of the burning ship and the woman in white. I supposed Lily had heard it as a child, but, like me, had only half believed it. Now, having had it retold by Archie and given a new and contemporary twist, she was clearly spooked - though, now, I could see, comforted by Jack's obvious disbelief, his attributing the story to one more of Archie's bizarre flights of fancy - a tall tale, a more than usually outrageous one.

* * *

At the end of the lobster season, I happened to be on the fishing boat that was returning Archie and his four-wheeler to the mainland. Jack had already hauled our boat and, since I needed to lay in a supply of staple groceries, I'd begged a ride from Angus, a fisherman I scarcely knew. He is a man of *very* few words, and I have always thought he didn't much care to waste them on women - well, on me anyway. In twenty years he and I had scarcely exchanged more than the most minimal greetings on the wharf.

Suddenly, now, all at once, as soon as we left the island harbor, I could feel that Angus was working up to having some sort of say.

Archie and I were sitting side by side on the wooden bench in the very small cabin. Gus was at the helm. I figured he was going to talk to Archie, but I was wrong: his words were directed to me.

"Hear you've got a lot of them funny stripy brown snakes down to your place," he began.

"Yes, a few," I said, racking my brains to think of a way of changing the subject because I know that just the mention of a snake is almost more than Archie can bear. It's his weak spot: his phobia, I suppose you'd call it these days.

But Gus was not to be deterred.

"Up 'round the house, and down the path to the pond too, aren't they?" he insisted.

"Um...mm....," I grunted, hoping that the strident hum of the motor would prevent this conversation from continuing. I couldn't disagree with Gus, though. Those odd-colored striped brown and beige snakes were all over the place. I suppose they look different from their mainland cousins because they've been on the island for who knows how long. Way before people. Sort of a Maritime version of Darwin's Galapagos reptiles, I've thought. Not found elsewhere.

But Gus, the man who I thought never spoke unless he had to, was carrying on this conversation with hardly any assistance from me.

"I never went down there no more after what Clyde saw just next your place ... in Duncan and Mary's field when them was haying."

Curious, I fell for his bait. "So, what did Clyde see?" I found myself asking.

"Well, he saw the mother of all snakes. S'pose it was that sea serpent from the pond. She come writhin' up outa the reeds and 'crost the end of the hayfield. All fifteen feet of her, if there was an inch ... some thick too...." Gus paused for effect before continuing. "Clyde, he's my cousin, you know, said he never waited around to see where the critter went. Just hightailed it outa there...."

Gus turned to look at Archie, which made me turn sideways too. Archie was a pale greenish color. He was trying to stand up, but was defeated by the descent of the boat into a deep trough. Finally he got up and made it to the cabin door and out onto the deck - apparently unmindful of the driving rain and heavy swell.

Gus glanced back at me with what I'd swear was an incredibly jubilant look.

"Never knew Archie got sea sick," he said. A few seconds later, straight-faced by then, he added, "Just goes to show you don't it. Never kid a kidder."

THE INTERVIEW

Adrian and I are off to interview the lightkeeper on Rocky Island. Since he - the lightkeeper, that is - is representative of a vanishing breed, an anachronism in a world where most lights in current shipping lanes have long since been computerized, I thought an interview featuring this man's life and work might provide a welcome diversion for the somewhat jaded readers of the magazine which employs me. Although Carlyle, my editor, didn't seem much interested when I broached the idea, he finally said he would go along with it.

I guess I must have looked so unhappy about his initial unenthusiastic response that he later felt he had to come up with some kind words. "I've been thinking about your lightkeeper," he said, pausing by my desk. "Since your pieces are mostly winners, offbeat and intriguing," he went on, patting me lightly on the arm, "I think you'd better go for this one."

I'm never sure if Carlyle is really as keen on my work as he lets on or whether he just wants to keep in my good books because he likes me. Well, I suppose I'd have to admit that his feeling for me appears to be more than liking. I am fond of him too. But that's another story.

I know that Carlyle is not very pleased that Adrian is tagging along, and, truth to tell, I'm not much in favour of this turn of events either, although our reasons are not the same. But Adrian is very hard to put off once he has his sights fixed on something. This aggressiveness may be the secret of his success in his business relationships, but it has been getting me down for some time now. He considers himself an authority on nearly everything, and pontificates at length.

Four months ago when I first met Adrian, I was impressed with his seeming insights into so many disparate subjects, but now, since he has begun to advise and criticize me about not only the topics I choose for my articles but my literary style too, I find myself going to all sorts of lengths to avoid showing him my copy before it's in print. It is not as if he had any flair for writing, and, now that I am sure that this is so, I have begun to wonder how right he is about other things - things I don't pretend to know much about.

*   *   *

Since Rocky Island is only three miles offshore, Adrian imagines that getting there and back will be quick and easy, but I suspect he is wrong about this. Although I have warned him that an undertaking of this sort is unlikely to go smoothly, I realize he hasn't listened. I have done a lot of islanding, and, rewarding as I have found most of these excursions, *quick* and *easy* are *not* words I would ever choose to describe them: such trips tend to be fraught with unexpected and time-consuming complications. I find that is partly what makes them interesting, though I realize that most people would likely not agree with me.

The fisherman I went to see a couple of weeks ago when I first conceived this idea agreed right away to take me to the island. "No problem," he said. "Just drop by when you're ready. I'll take you across and come back for you. I'm not fishing all this month, so I'll be free."

Because of my lifelong acquaintance with fishermen and their ways, I was perfectly satisfied with the verbal agreement I had made with this young man. But whereas I am used to such seemingly casual arrangements when planning trips to island destinations, Adrian is not.

As soon as we left Halifax, he said, "Well, what time's our appointment with this fisherman? Hope you gave us lots of leeway. Looks like we might be running into fog."

So I have had to explain about the loose arrangement the fisherman and I have. I have been forced to admit that I don't have a specific appointment, not even a definite day. I haven't been able to convince Adrian that fishermen mostly refuse to be tied down in advance because everything depends on how the weather seems to be shaping up just as you're set to embark. I have explained that, although their lives are unlike other people's, governed by different rules, they are more dependable than most.

Adrian clearly doesn't believe me. He has gone from unrestrained fury to a seething and repressed anger. "You mean," he says between clenched teeth, "that this drive might be for nothing, that we mightn't even get across to the island?"

I nod, and then, realizing that he can't - or won't - look at me, murmur, "Unhuh. That's possible."

Suddenly Adrian accelerates into the fog, hoping, I suspect, to punish me for what I know he considers to be my ridiculous approach to this outing. I think right now he wouldn't much mind if we hit something. That would serve me right, I suppose he imagines. So this is road rage, I tell myself incredulously. I am not impressed. Mostly though, I am terrified, a terrified hostage.

* * *

When by some miracle we reach our destination, my fisherman greets us laconically and, in short order, steers us down the wharf and onto his Cape Islander.

Adrian asks about the fog, which is now very dense. I find it ironic that Adrian is so concerned about the fog over the water when he drove blindly, recklessly, through the fog on the road.

"Fog's no problem," my fisherman says.

I believe him. He has his Loran-C to steer by. As well, I feel he knows what he is about. When I first talked to him, he told me he had been fishing this stretch of the Nova Scotia coast with his father and brothers since he was ten. I'd guess he is now about twenty-eight, windburned and muscular, and on his own. He is, however, no longer the outgoing fellow he was when I came here alone. I expect Adrian's glowering countenance has dampened his spirits as much as it has mine.

It turns out that Adrian is not only unfamiliar with boats, but leery of them. I realize this at once by the way he climbs so slowly down the slippery iron rungs on the wharf and steps gingerly onto the boat. Although it's a dead calm, he acts as if he thinks the boat is about to sink under us.

Secretly, I find I am not displeased. Serves him right, I think, for almost frightening me to death on the highway. And then I am appalled by the vindictive streak I see rising up in myself.

It is hard to tell what my fisherman - Ron, he says his name is - thinks of us, although I suspect his opinion of me is much diminished by the fact that I have Adrian in tow. Well, if that is so, his viewpoint pretty much jibes with my own just now.

As we head out into the fog, Adrian's uneasiness increases, so that it begins to affect me. Now it is not anger which radiates from him, but fear. He hasn't said a word since we climbed aboard, which, considering his usual garrulousness, is amazing. The eerie stillness is broken only by the hum of the motor and the echoing calls of invisible seabirds.

Suddenly shots sound close at hand. We seem to have entered a war zone. I am shaken, trembling. Being a war correspondent has never appealed to me.

I glance up at Ron's back, looking for some manifestation of distress - but finding none. He appears oblivious to the shots. His broad shoulders are still in the same relaxed position.

I stand up and take a couple of steps to where he is astride at the wheel. He nods to acknowledge my approach, but does not speak. I cannot contain my fear and shout out over the drumming of the motor, "What's all that about?"

"Oh, just some of the guys duck hunting, I imagine," he replies casually.

"But how could they be? It isn't the season, is it? Anyhow, they couldn't see anything through this fog," I call out, my voice sounding shrill and strained to my own ears.

Ron does not respond to my comment about out-of-season hunting, attempting only to clarify why shots might be fired on such a foggy day.

"S'pose they found a clear patch," he tells me evenly. He doesn't seem worried that shots might go astray, that we might be hit.

Despite Ron's composure, I am not convinced that we are safe. I cower beside Adrian on the narrow cabin bench.

But there are no more shots and soon we are alongside the island wharf, a much smaller and more run-down version of the one we left behind on the mainland. Ron does not cut the motor and tie up. He helps us onto the droplet-covered rungs leading up to the wharf and hands up our knapsacks. Then he is off. "See you before sundown," he shouts back.

What sun? I wonder. So far today is shaping up as my very worst ever island venture. If it were possible to go back, I would go. The last thing I feel like doing is interviewing anyone.

* * *

"So, where's the lighthouse?" Adrian asks promptly.

"At the other end of the island," I reply meekly, and then add, "But the island is small. We only have to walk a couple of miles."

Adrian is incredulous. "Walk? ... And then we'll have to walk another couple of miles to get back here?"

"Right," I say, not very meekly this time. "You can stay here and wait for Ron to return," I suggest, hoping now that he will do just that. And then I can't help adding, "Remember, I warned you this likely wasn't going to be a quick and easy trip. You didn't listen."

Catching the note of faint menace in my voice - a sound I don't recall hearing there myself until now - Adrian picks up his already damp knapsack, hands me mine, and begins walking quickly down the wharf towards ghostly tree shapes which gradually emerge from the fog. I trot alongside, trying to keep up, concerned that if I hurry too much I may slip on the slick boards.

A narrow gravel road - scarcely more than a path - leads away from the wharf and into the woods. It looks just wide enough for a half-ton truck. There is no room to pass, but I suppose that one half-ton and maybe a four-wheeler are the only vehicles on the island. Outcroppings of jagged rock make the road treacherous. Whoever drives along here will have to manoeuver slowly and carefully.

Although Adrian and I are now scarcely on speaking terms, I begin to relax under the spell of this tranquil place. Tall spruces, like those which were starkly marshalled along the shore are now interspersed with birches and a few maples. The birches are enveloped in a haze of new green. The maples, less advanced, are festooned with rosy flowers. On the branches of both warblers are busily feasting on whatever it is they're finding to eat. And although we could reach out and touch some of these colorful small birds, they are not alarmed. Indeed, they appear impervious to our presence. They are, I suppose, too intent on stocking up for the next leg of their northward migration to give us the time of day. Two sentinel ravens watch us from a dead branch, more with curiosity I think than alarm. A rabbit runs across the road a few feet ahead of us. He is pursued by a fox. They disappear through the banks of narcissi which border the road. Since these flowers cannot be indigenous, I begin to wonder about the man or woman who planted the bulbs from which they spring. That must have been long ago; maybe a couple of centuries, I think. No one could afford so many bulbs today. Perhaps there were just a few at first - a few which naturalized more successfully than any I have planted in my own island garden. Or maybe, I think, mine have not been in place long enough.

The charm and peacefulness of this isolated spot seem to have had a soothing effect on Adrian too. "Well, this isn't so bad," he says. Then immediately, like a child who thinks he should still be sulking, he shuts up again. But I am aware that he seems unable to hold onto his dark mood any more than I can.

"You know, I'm hungry already," I say. "I hope we brought enough food."

Out of the corner of my eye, I see that Adrian is considering this subject with some interest.

"I think maybe we should eat before we get there," he suggests presently. "When we're in sight of the place, you know. What do you think?"

"Sounds good to me," I say.

So that is what we do. We have our picnic within sight of the lighthouse and the keeper's white, two story, shuttered dwelling. We sit on boulders while we eat and speculate about the place and its inhabitants.

"Children live here," I observe, pointing to two small bicycles leaning against a shed.... "Their garden plot is tiny, isn't it?" I remark next after a moment's silence. "Too little you'd think, wouldn't you, to provide much food for the four people who must live here?"

"True," says Adrian, who is pouring himself another cup of coffee from the thermos. "But look at those piles of stones." He points to a huge heap. "Imagine the work someone had clearing them out of a patch even so small as this one."

I nod and we both consider the rockiness of the terrain here on the high cliff above the sea. Our walk from the wharf has been a gradual uphill trudge. The ground on the other end of the island, where we landed, looked fairly fertile I think: well, fertile compared to this anyway. Here, there are not even any trees. I remark that I find this part of the island not unlike Baffin Island. I tell Adrian that it reminds me of the way the land around Pangnirtung looked when Carlyle sent me there to do an article - even to the blueberry bushes clinging to pockets of earth between the rocks. I do not proceed with this analogy: Adrian is not listening.

*   *   *

The keeper and his wife seem delighted to see us. When the woman opens the door, I see that there are five children, not two, grouped around the kitchen table. The younger two appear to be about five and seven. The bicycles we spotted must be theirs.

It is clear that, like us, the family has just finished lunch. They offer us some of their leftover rhubarb crisp. Adrian accepts this appetizing dessert happily, washing it down with a bottle of homebrew the keeper wants him to try.

Almost at once Adrian and the lightkeeper launch into a conversation about the hockey playoffs. I dismiss the idea of interrupting, realizing how unwelcome my suggestion of an interview would be right now. Besides, the keeper's wife - Nadine, she tells me her name is - is trying to get my attention. She has made a comment which I have not grasped because I just heard the keeper offer Adrian a tour of the lighthouse. They are out of the house and across the yard while I am racking my brains for a polite excuse to join them.

But I have to admit defeat. I know perfectly well they do not want me tagging along. It also appears that Nadine has set her sights on having a heart-to-heart conversation with me. She tells the three older children to do the dishes and sends the younger two outside to play. She ushers me into the living room.

Having made these practical arrangements, Nadine tells me that Adrian and I are the season's first visitors and that, although she loves her island life, visitors - especially the earliest ones - are a treat.

"Funny, unpredictable things often happen when they come," she says smiling, recollecting. "Like the time a couple of years ago when a whole boatload came over for a Canada Day picnic. It rained on the way over and some of the crowd got wet. One woman who hadn't brought a jacket or a raincoat was absolutely soaked, so I lent her one of my dresses. When she went outside, Charles - that's my husband - came up behind her, thinking she was me and gave her a great big hug. He was so embarrassed when she turned around.... We've been laughing about that ever since.

"But winter here is lovely too," she continues. "We snow-shoe and cross country ski. We make music and play games in the evening. And then there are the wonderful storms. I wish you could see them. It's worth climbing to the top of the light-house to watch. The children and I often do that. When it's really wild, the sea throws rocks up over the cliff into our yard.... As if we don't have enough already," she laughs. A few have even hit the front of the house. It's amazing that we haven't had any broken windows. Not yet, anyway."

These are not events which entertain the rest of the contemporary world, I think. And yet Nadine is clearly not simple-minded. She expresses herself well. I listen to what she has to say, resigned to accepting the situation I find myself in with as good grace as possible.

*   *   *

It takes me a while to realize that time spent with Nadine does not constitute martyrdom for me. Not only is Nadine intelligent and lively, fun to be with, but I begin to think that she is perhaps the most remarkable person I have ever met.

I learn that she and Charles have seven children, not five; that the two eldest are at Harvard on full scholarships; that she has home-schooled all the children; that she was born on this light station where her father, grandfather and great-grand-father were keepers; that when Charles was sick for three years a while back she ran the light station on her own.

While we chat, my eyes rove around the room. No ordinary living room this: an art gallery really. Transfixed by the painting opposite the couch on which I sit, I begin to lose track of what Nadine is telling me about the lighthouse, its history and maintenance. I am aware at the back of my mind that this is why I have come here and that I should be paying attention. But the paintings are captivating - delicate yet powerful watercolors which cannot be ignored. They demand all my attention.

I stare at an ancient stone lighthouse, its light shining palely through a blizzard. A lean old man, oilskin clad and carrying a lantern is just opening an immense, heavy door. A portal would be a better designation: this building looks old-world. I wonder how the old man has the strength to open such a door. I sense a story here. I turn to Nadine who is watching my reaction with interest. I do not have to ask for an explanation. She guesses what I want to hear.

"That is my great-grandfather outside the old lighthouse, the one the government people tore down long before I was born. He has spotted a vessel in trouble and is going to the cove to launch the lifeboat. He plans to wait in the lee of the building for his students to put on their gear and come and help him."

"How do you know all this?" I ask.

"Well," Nadine explains, "I've pierced the facts together from old letters and clippings, as well as from my father's and grandfather's stories, to come up with this interpretation. As I told you before, this light station has been in the hands of my father's people for at least as far back as my great-grandfather's time.

"I have heard lots of stories about this old lighthouse. It was huge and meticulously constructed by Scottish stonemasons. The walls were supposedly three feet thick to withstand attacks by lawless seafarers. There were slits in the walls to let in the light, so it must have looked a little like a medieval fortress. Only the door would admit anyone, and even it was heavy oak, and metal studded.

"The building was large enough to house not only the light and the paraphernalia necessary to maintain it, but accommodated the keeper and his family as well as a half dozen or so young men attending a navigation school which great-grandfather ran during the winter. He was their only instructor and apparently an excellent one. Those boys - they were only fourteen to sixteen - helped great-grandfather in emergencies. When they 'graduated' they apparently got superior postings on important vessels."

I find this story amazing, but it is still the painting which enthralls me. "But tell me," I ask, "who painted this wonderful picture? I feel as if I could step right into it.... I suppose it was a remarkable painter who got shipwrecked here in your great-grandfather's day - a man of Audubon's talent whose fixation was on this place rather than birds."

Nadine laughs.

"Oh, I painted that," she says. "It's my visual rendition of the old facts.... And there on the wall behind you is the cove and the old lifeboat. We keep a smaller boat there now. That cove's where the children learned to swim."

"And the road?" I ask, pointing to the watercolor next to the cove painting. "It looks so intriguing. Where does it lead?"

"Oh, that's the road down to the cove. Well, It's hardly more than a trail.... As you'll see when you look around, I have a fixation on pathways. The less travelled, the more they interest me."

"Yes, I see," I say, contemplating other nearby paintings. "Some of the roads - paths - are almost overgrown. But they're not all on the island, are they?"

"Oh yes," Nadine explains, "all the paintings in this room are of the island. The scenes here are the ones I *have* to paint."

I recognize the rocky road Adrian and I walked along to get here. Two children - Nadine's two youngest, I think - are riding their bikes. They have their backs to the artist.

"You mostly do landscapes," I comment.

"Not really," she says. "I've done a lot of the children. The dining room and the upstairs hall and bedrooms are full of family portraits. I've nearly run out of space though," she notes thoughtfully.

"To make more room you could sell a few of these wonderful works," I suggest. "I am sure buyers would snap them up if they could see them."

By Nadine's smile I realize she knows that this is so.

"Probably. I do sell a few. In the summers when visitors come. This fall I am supposed to have an exhibition in Cambridge.

"I think I mentioned that our two eldest are there - at Harvard. They have brought back friends, one of them an artist. Then, late last summer a gallery curator came and talked about my having a show and sale down there.

"But we're having trouble trying to decide which paintings we are willing to part with. Each of the children and Charles have different favorites, and I find I'm not very good at duplicating the ones they want to keep. Whatever went into them in the first place seems to reside in the original painting. Funny thing ..." she says dreamily, "I keep wondering why this is so.

"All these scenes are so much a part of our lives here - the only part we'll be able to take with us when we leave."

I am jolted out of my contemplation of these landscapes and dreamscapes. I realize what Nadine is driving at. After all, I remind myself, that is why I am here; to report on the running of one of our last light stations and its imminent demise. I feel too sad to speak.

"Yes, this station is closing this fall," Nadine says unhappily. "We'll have to leave the island."

* * *

By the end of the afternoon I have all the material I need - and more - for my article. Not what I expected. Better. Much better. I am grateful to the powers-that-be for granting me the opportunity to talk with Nadine rather than her husband.

But I am moved by this revelation of Nadine and her family's life far beyond the demands of my job. My curiosity, my desire for an interview, seem shallow now. Deeper feelings are involved. What I have seen and heard here this afternoon has, it seems to me, changed my perspectives permanently.

When Adrian and I say good-bye to Nadine and Charles and begin walking back to the wharf, I am in a mellow and charitable mood. I am even prepared to forgive Adrian for jinxing my plan to interview the keeper. Nevertheless, since I am still mulling over my afternoon's experiences, I do not feel like talking. Adrian chats away cheerily, but I am only half listening.

HONORARY ABORIGINAL

As far back as I can remember, my Aunt Marni and her children were caught up in one crisis after another. It was her husband Basil - my uncle through marriage, not blood - who precipitated each of these unsettling events.

I am convinced that Uncle Basil never meant to throw a wrench into the works. It's just that he has rarely listened to what other people say, or, to be more precise, he has only *partly* tuned in to what he is being told, a state of affairs which has invariably led to more upsets than if he had not listened at all.

For years my mother, Marni's older sister, kept telling my father that she didn't know how Marni could put up with her lot. The frequent, surprising and disturbing consequences of Uncle Basil's idiosyncrasies left poor Marni, my mother insisted, with virtually no control over her life.

"My mother's refrain, aired on numerous occasions and punctuated by substantial pauses, went something like this: "If Marni didn't have the patience of Job, she'd have thrown over the traces years ago.... I suppose, though, she feels she has to stay on account of the children.... And, truth to tell, Basil hasn't been a bad provider.... He can be quite a charmer too.... On first acquaintance.... That's before you realize he's so much on his own frequency, so absorbed in his own agenda that he doesn't seem able to remember other people's."

Then she'd add when she thought I was out of earshot, "But what really puzzles me is why Meredith is always clamoring to visit over there. In that house you just never know what might happen next."

What my mother didn't understand was that it was precisely this total unpredictability at my closest relatives' house which lured me there. Almost everything which occurred in that ramshackle hillside mansion was in such contrast to what I then considered the boring sameness of my own well-ordered home where it seemed to me that nothing out of the way ever happened.

Now though, I can see that what, early on, appeared to me to be hilarious mixups must never have seemed comical from my Aunt Marni's perspective. Besides, with the passing of time, I began to realize that Uncle Basil's eccentricities were becoming more pronounced and more bizarre - and, when viewed from close up and over the long-term, perhaps not so amusing. Well, not when they affected you personally, as they did me during my last year of school, the winter I lived in that crazy house. By my graduation day, I found myself reluctantly agreeing with my mother's assessment of Marni's disastrous domestic setup. Not that I told my mother then that I had begun to agree with her pronouncements.

So when, the day after my graduation and my two younger cousins', Aunt Marni finally opted for a dramatic change, I realized that the leap she made was long overdue. What took me ages to come to terms with was the amazing and radical nature of this leap. I understand now, though, that what Uncle Basil did that graduation day - and the months preceding it - was enough to produce a spectacular reaction in almost anyone. For Aunt Marni it must have been, as my mother said, *the last straw* - and, for my mother, shades of her own traumatic graduation day, only worse, because, as my mother pointed out, Marni was trapped and she hadn't been.

My mother's disenchantment with Uncle Basil and his unpredictable habits began long before he married her sister. She and Basil had been at school together for all twelve years and he had agreed to escort her to the graduation dance.

Basil, though, apparently had other things on his mind that day. He had spent the afternoon delivering furniture his father had made and he had stayed for supper and cards that evening at a client's house. When he walked home long after dark, he forgot his father's horse - still in the shafts and attached to the delivery wagon. Mrs. Polley had had to telephone and ask him to come back for this rig and the poor animal which drew it. (By the following week Basil's father had purchased a secondhand half-ton for future furniture deliveries.)

Meanwhile, Basil had apparently never thought about the graduation and dance he had missed. Well, that was until my grandmother went over and lit into him the next morning. Forty years later, and well into her eighties, Gram is still furious about what happened that day and never seems to tire of re-hashing its ins and outs. She's told me repeatedly that Basil just stood there like a post, saying nothing. "No apology. No explanation. Nothing.... Not a single reaction like a normal person."

She said she told Basil that standing my mother up for that important dance was the next worst thing to leaving a girl at the altar. Though years later when Basil married Marni, who had been only eight at the time of that infamous graduation, I imagine Gram wished he hadn't turned up.

This first graduation fiasco was only the beginning of my mother's and grandmother's exasperation with Basil. After a while, though, my mother was ready to declare a truce. And by the time she had married my father, she had pretty much forgiven him. By and large, her life was working out well and she had lots more important things on her mind than Basil - two year old me, for instance.

Since Basil is really quite an exceptional furniture maker, having benefited from his father's expert tutelage, my mother decided to ask him to make a maple colonial settee and end tables for the new house she and my father had had built. Basil had seemed to listen to her explanation, according to Gram, who by then had moved in with my parents. Gram vowed that Basil had even jotted down notes.

But when he had delivered the furniture, the settee and end tables were cherry, not maple, and the style Danish Modern. Someone suggested later that, because the Justafsons had gotten Basil to make their Danish Modern furniture just before my mother put in her order, he had either developed a preference for this style or simply couldn't see the point in turning out the elaborate spindles which the colonial assignment would have entailed. Or maybe he had just forgotten, had lost the notes he had taken down. Since Basil never explained, his rationale, if he had one, was anybody's guess.

I can't understand why my mother accepted the substitutes. Although these pieces are attractive and very well made, Scandinavian furniture didn't, and still doesn't, go with anything else in the house.

That's been one of the amazing things about Basil: he has managed to do exactly as he pleases and get away with it. His whims rarely seemed to trigger the kind of repercussions anyone else's similar deviations would produce. Well, not until Aunt Marni *took the bit between her teeth and made a run for it,* to quote my mother again.

Even nowadays when Basil mostly builds houses instead of furniture, he hardly ever, as far as I know, constructs them according to the prospective buyer's specifications. And I've heard that, if anyone remonstrates, he just stands still as a post, as he did when my grandmother first berated him. The strangest thing of all is that his customers continue to put up with such outrageous behavior, paying up and moving into houses unlike the ones they had had in mind. Afterwards, if the subject is under discussion, the buyer, if pushed, will tell his friends something like this: "Oh well, the price was right, and it's not so bad. We're getting used to it."

Still, none of Basil's customers really wants to talk about their dealings with him. I think maybe they can't figure out exactly how Basil got the upper hand, without apparently saying a word - and I suppose they are embarrassed.

*   *   *

I was eight when I was first allowed to spend the night with my cousins - three girls; one my age, one nine months younger and one a year older - in their immense room under the eaves, a room with three double beds a good twelve feet apart and huge walk-in closets, which we pretended were inhabited by all sorts of fantastic beings, though only mice were visible.

That evening after supper was over, the dishes done and the kitchen tidy, Aunt Marni told Uncle Basil and us children that she was going next door to quilt and that she would be back about nine. We were, she said, to go to bed at eight. Uncle Basil was to make sure of that.

Not a complicated arrangement, one would think. Who could imagine anything going wrong? Well, perhaps only someone who knew Uncle Basil well.

Apart from her reminder about our bedtime, Aunt Marni made one other parting comment through the screen door as it came to behind her. "Basil," I heard her call out, "I've left peas soaking in that dish on the counter. They're for tomorrow's soup, so don't pour off the water.... Remember!"

Now, although I thought at the time that these instructions were simple and easy to follow - even for an eight year old - Uncle Basil managed to complicate them in a way I suspect no one else could have.

First of all, as soon as Aunt Marni was out of sight, Uncle Basil went right out to the garden and planted the peas - though I didn't know this until the next day. That was because my cousins - Julie, Annie and Andrea - and I, along with two of the neighbor's girls, Cynthia and Myrtle, were playing hide-and-seek in the woods behind the barn.

By a quarter to eight we were all hot and bothered, covered by mosquito bites too, so we went into the kitchen for the milk and cookies Aunt Marni had left for us. We had just finished the last cookie when Uncle Basil came in from his workshop and told us it was bedtime.

Everything seemed normal until Cynthia and Myrtle turned to go home.

"Hey there," Uncle Basil bellowed as they were about to open the screen door, "didn't I tell you it's bedtime? Run along now like good girls. The others are already on their way upstairs."

This was a long speech for Uncle Basil, and Cynthia and Myrtle were intimidated by his booming voice and commanding manner as he issued this ultimatum. Since I was sitting on the bottom step, I tiptoed through the hall to the kitchen door and beckoned to Cynthia and Myrtle. With tears streaming down their cheeks, they followed me.

"Come on upstairs," I whispered. "Aunt Marni will be home soon and she'll straighten things out. Annie says she always checks to make sure everyone's all right."

When Uncle Basil poked his head into the big attic room

about 8:30, all six of us were in bed pretending sleep - two to each of the three double beds. Since the three beds were all occupied as usual, their double occupancy mustn't have registered. Apparently satisfied, Uncle Basil turned and trudged back down the two flights of stairs.

I began to giggle. Soon my cousins joined in, and finally Cynthia and Myrtle's sobs became gasps of laughter. None of us could stop, until we heard a stamping of heavy boots on the porch and pounding on the front door. Now silence reigned in the big room. The six of us tiptoed to the open windows, but, on account of the porch roof, we couldn't see a thing. We could hear well enough, though.

Two men were questioning Uncle Basil. Their strong voices were borne up clearly to our windows.

"We just got a call about two little girls gone missing," one of them said tentatively. "They didn't turn up at home when they was supposed to. You haven't by any chance seen any extra kids, have you?"

No sound we could hear from Uncle Basil. Probably, Annie whispered, he was shaking his head. Or maybe he just said *no* and we couldn't hear.

"Their names are Myrtle and Cynthia Justafson," the other man said. "From next door there.... Their mother said they were over playing with your girls earlier. Is that right?"

"Don't know. Mine are in bed and asleep," Uncle Basil mumbled as he shut the door.

When the two men emerged from under the porch roof, we saw that they were the town's two policemen. One of them, Mr. Collins, kept scratching his head and looking back at our house. Both walked slowly and seemed puzzled.

Just as they reached the end of the flagstone walk and were opening the gate, Aunt Marni appeared on the other side. She seemed in a hurry. She and the policemen conferred briefly.

They all looked worried, but since they were out of earshot now we couldn't hear what was being said.

Soon afterwards, we heard Aunt Marni on the stairs. We had just time to jump back into bed. Naturally at a glance she saw the two extra children, now unsure about whether to cry or laugh.

It was Annie, my eldest cousin, who explained what had happened - and asked if Cynthia and Myrtle could stay the night, seeing as how they were already in bed.

I got the feeling that Aunt Marni thought it would be a good idea if they stayed. My guess was that she didn't want to try to smuggle Cynthia and Myrtle past Uncle Basil. I think we all realized that, since he likely wouldn't listen to an explanation, his reaction was impossible to predict.

Aunt Marni said she'd do what she could to fix things. We watched her hurrying back down the path and along the sidewalk to the Justafsons. Later we learned she'd explained to Mrs. Justafson that, since Myrtle and Cynthia were safely in bed, there wasn't much point in disturbing them. Mrs. Justafson phoned the police to say that the lost children had been found and Aunt Marni rushed back to let us know that our friends could stay overnight.

*   *   *

Though that evening's events were memorable for me, I realize now that for Aunt Marni they must have been a turning point. Convinced after this episode that her husband was totally unaware of how many children were supposed to be in the house, that fall she began bringing home a neglected child or two from the remedial classes she volunteered with at the school. She'd explain to the parents, the teachers and to us that Alma or Jonathan - or whoever - needed extra help, which anyone could see was true. It was also perfectly clear that Aunt Marni was exceptionally good with these children. They flourished under her tutelage. That *patience of Job* which my mother had talked about was just what they needed; that, together with Marni's special insights into other people's feelings.

What was a surprise to everyone, though, was that Uncle Basil also contributed amazingly to Aunt Marni's star boarders' well-being. He treated the visiting children like his own. That is, he mostly ignored them. Actually, he probably thought they *were* his, if he thought about them at all. He didn't ask them any embarrassing questions. Well, he didn't ask them any questions at all, since he didn't seem to recognize them as strangers. And when they left, *cured*, so to speak, their departure - and their replacements' arrival - made no stir either.

So gradually Aunt Marni opened up, cleaned, aired and repapered the unused bedrooms on the second floor, along the hall from the master bedroom she and Uncle Basil shared. She wanted the *problem children*, as they had been labelled at school, nearby so that, if they woke troubled in the night, she could hear them and go scurrying in to comfort them.

My cousins, and I when I visited, still slept in that wonderful attic room. Though by the time I came to stay that last winter when my mother was too sick to cope at home, I was given a room of my own on the second floor. By then Annie had graduated from school and was training as a nurse. Only one of Aunt Marni's protégées remained in the house. This one, Priscilla, had taken all her spare time for four years. Small wonder.

*   *   *

Priscilla, who, according to her aunt, had been named after Priscilla Presley, was blind and an orphan. She had lived almost since her birth with her maternal grandmother, a Mi'kmaq elder, who, wanting to protect her from the world at large, had avoided sending her to school. The grandmother had undoubtedly been right: no one at our small school was equipped to deal with a blind child - and even the visiting special education teacher didn't know braille. The school board wasn't about to hire anyone who did. *Think of the money it would cost for just one child*, they rationalized.

Then one Saturday morning, Priscilla's aunt had turned up at Aunt Marni's house. She'd heard about the wonders Aunt Marni had worked with other handicapped children and begged her to help Priscilla.

Aunt Marni's answer must have been *yes*, because the next thing we knew, Priscilla was put up in the best of the revitalized second floor bedrooms and Aunt Marni was learning braille - and Mi'kmaq. By this time, I was about fourteen. Priscilla was seven.

When Priscilla arrived at Aunt Marni's she couldn't do much for herself. Her grandmother had felt so sorry for the child that she had waited on her hand and foot. Putting on her snowsuit and tying her shoes were tasks Priscilla had never tried, tasks which Aunt Marni, for all her tender-heartedness, insisted Priscilla learn right away. Priscilla cried a lot those first days. The new demands overwhelmed her. My cousins and I were betting that this venture would never work out.

That was before Aunt Marni got Priscilla to teach her Mi'kmaq; and since at first Aunt Marni made a lot of mistakes, including, it seems, some real gaffes, Priscilla cheered up, even laughing out loud at some of Aunt Marni's most outrageous pronunciations.

Most evenings, after Priscilla was in bed, Aunt Marni got out the brailler which the Institute for the Blind had lent her, together with a home study course from the same source. She'd

learn enough each evening to help Priscilla with her letters and
easy words the next day. Pretty soon, it was hard to tear Priscilla
- or Aunt Marni - away from their work. Both of them seemed
happy.

*   *   *

By the time Julie, Andrea and I were in Grade 12 - Julie,
because her birthday was in November, so she'd started school
at five instead of six - Priscilla lived permanently at Aunt Marni
and Uncle Basil's. Her grandmother had died by then and her
aunt was crippled with arthritis, so I think Aunt Marni adopted
Priscilla, though I'm not sure. Anyway, Priscilla had been calling Aunt Marni *Mom* for years, so whether the adoption was
official or not, the relationship had long since been emotionally
cemented.

At the start of that final year at school, Julie, Andrea
and I had applied to a number of universities. Since we were all
better than average students, we had high hopes of being accepted at the college of our choice. We thought we might be
eligible for scholarships too, particularly Julie who, despite the
fact that she was younger than the rest of us, had led the class.
She had shown herself to be really brilliant - and she didn't
even have to study much. The principal and guidance teacher
thought she should apply to a few world class universities -
Harvard, for instance, along with other prestigious universities
outside the Maritimes.

But as the year went by and most of our classmates got
acceptances - or rejections - neither Andrea, Julie nor I received
a single reply. When, by the end of April, we still hadn't heard,
our principal decided to contact some of the schools to which
we had applied.

As it turned out, we had been accepted at several of our

chosen places and Julie at all, including Harvard. When they were contacted, the registrars said they'd written months ago to let us know, and, when they hadn't heard back, had concluded that we had made other plans. They had given our spots to students who were next in line.

* * *

What we eventually learned was that Uncle Basil had thrown out these acceptance letters. When Aunt Marni tackled him on the subject, he finally admitted that he must have disposed of them, thinking they were more junk mail. He apparently defended this action by saying that there's been an awful lot of junk mail over the preceding six months, and although he had told the postmistress to throw out unsolicited mail - flyers and suchlike - he said he thought she'd forgotten. So, when he saw all the strange addresses in the left hand corners of the college envelopes, he said he supposed he'd gotten rid of them. Apparently, he hadn't been apologetic, just matter-of-fact.

It was hard for me to believe that Uncle Basil had actually tried to explain himself. That must have been because even he could see that Aunt Marni was on the rampage and he'd better try to salvage their former comfortable, for him, relationship. This was not to be.

"So that's what happened to all those important letters. You've ruined the children's future. You're an impossible man. I'm not going to put up with you much longer."

We were in the hall when Aunt Marni delivered this ultimatum in the kitchen. Despite the seriousness of the situation, none of us could believe our ears. The impossible had happened. Aunt Marni, for the first time, as far as anyone knew, had lost her temper, laid down the law, and given every indication that she was prepared to stand her ground.

"And I suppose you threw out my invitation to Marian's wedding too. No one understood when I didn't at least acknowledge it and send a present."

Uncle Basil didn't seem to reply to that charge. At least we didn't hear him say anything. I got the impression, though, that in this instance his keeping mum wasn't going to work. It also seemed to me that now that Aunt Marni had taken a stand, she would not back down.

* * *

Uncle Basil didn't come to our graduation exercises. Since he hadn't gone to Annie's the year before either, we didn't expect him to turn up. So that wasn't what finished Uncle Basil and Aunt Marni's disintegrating relationship. It was what happened just as Aunt Marni, Julie, Andrea and I returned from the ceremony that was *the last straw.* (My mother's assessment again.)

When the four of us opened the front door, two people, a man and a woman who identified themselves as census commissioners when Uncle Basil seemed unaware of the need to introduce them, were just about to leave. They explained that they'd only a couple more blanks to fill in on the form which Uncle Basil, as titular head of the house, had misplaced. (We could all guess where he had *misplaced* it.)

While Andrea, Julie and I charged upstairs to change, Aunt Marni went into the kitchen to start supper. The next day we learned that, while she was putting her apron on over her good dress and exhuming casseroles from the fridge, she'd overheard the final part of Uncle Basil's interview with the census takers.

According to my mother, in whom Aunt Marni had confided that evening, this is in essence what took place in the front hall: "So you say your wife is part Indian. Her grandfather a former chief in northern Manitoba? So she's got aboriginal blood? Right?"

"Right," Uncle Basil had replied.

By the time this exchange had sunk in to Aunt Marni's consciousness, the census commissioners were hurrying down the walk. That was when Aunt Marni had tackled Uncle Basil about giving them false information. Basil, though, had insisted, Marni told my mother, that he was absolutely correct, that she'd told him ages before that her grandfather was a Manitoba Indian chief.

"I did not *ever* say that," Aunt Marni had countered. "You only half listen to what I tell you. What I told you was that he was an HONORARY chief, that his farm adjoined the native people's lands, that he hunted with them and learned their language. BUT THE FACT IS THAT I DO NOT HAVE ANY NATIVE BLOOD IN MY VEINS, though truth to tell, I'd be quite happy if I had."

Anyhow, as my mother told Andrea, Julie and me the next day, Marni said she just couldn't get through to Basil. He had insisted he'd been right and thought he had the last word when he said, "Well, look at Priscilla. You can't tell me that child isn't Indian, and she's your daughter."

* * *

That evening when Uncle Basil was out in his workshop and we were at the graduation dance, Aunt Marni and Priscilla packed a small case each and went over to my parents' place. Mrs. Justafson drove them.

Next morning, before we could catch up with them, Aunt Marni and Priscilla were on their way West. My mother said their destination was Manitoba, up beyond Minnedosa, near the

Riding Mountains where our great-grandfather's farm had been.

My parents said they hadn't been able to persuade Marni to stay with them for a while. Marni had said she had to get away, far away, from Basil.

A week later, Andrea and I followed them. My mother had been quite insistent that we find Marni and Priscilla: she said she had to know that they were all right.

"It's such a crazy idea of Marni's," she said, "to go and find Grandfather's Indian band and offer her services to them. Living with Basil all those years must have addled her brains. You realize how long it's been since your great-grandfather farmed out there and hunted with the nearby native people?"

*   *   *

Since Andrea and I had planned to go and work on the West Coast for the year we had to put in before we could go to university, Manitoba wasn't exactly out of our way. Besides, we thought it would be an adventure, exciting to see our great-grandparents' farm too. We had never been out of the Maritimes before - except to Maine.

Julie wasn't with us: Harvard had come up with another offer of a place - with a full scholarship and work for the summer. I expect the powers that be there were impressed by what she'd accomplished already - having, for instance, aced two university correspondence courses (English and Math) while completing her grade twelve. By anyone's reckoning Julie's accomplishments were impressive.

When Andrea and I got to Minnedosa we cadged a ride with one of my mother's distant relatives to the reservation which was still where my mother had said it was. We found Marni and Priscilla right away. They'd been given a small house and already Marni had taken in another little girl about Priscilla's age who needed help.

A couple of neighbors were drinking tea with Marni at the kitchen table when we blew in. Marni acted as if she'd always lived there, always known these people. They seemed comfortable with her too.

Aunt Marni looked serene. Priscilla and her new roommate were sitting on the doorstep, talking and laughing, already friends.

After the visitors had gone, I asked Aunt Marni how she had managed to reestablish herself and Priscilla so quickly and amicably.

"Well," she began, "What happened was really quite amazing. When Priscilla and I arrived here, I tried to explain our coming to the first person I ran into, a grandmotherly person with a nice face and welcoming smile. She seemed to have some difficulty understanding me.... Not too surprising really," Marni laughed. "I was having some problems sorting things out myself.

"Anyhow, this old woman - maybe not much older than me -" (Marni laughed again) "took us to the Band Office and introduced us to the chief. I explained to him about my grandfather having been an honorary chief here, and tried to tell him that Priscilla and I would like to be part of this community.

"I figured he wasn't exactly taking in what I was saying. He had that peculiar look in his eyes that Basil got when I explained something to him - like some youngsters get in a math class when they can't understand an equation.

"Well, to cut a long story short, as they say, he took another look at Priscilla, who somehow knew he was staring in her direction and gave him one of her wonderful smiles, and then he said, "So your grandfather was chief here, eh? Welcome home then."

"And that was that. I tried again to explain about the

honorary part, but it seemed as if he wasn't tuned in, so it looks as if Priscilla and I are here to stay. I guess you could say I'm the second honorary aboriginal in this family."

DOWN RIVER COOK

Although cooking is **not** my vocation, it is an avocation which seems to please more people more consistently than almost anything else I do. No one finds fault with the food I prepare, or is one bit hesitant about consuming it, whereas, truth to tell, my other endeavors are not always greeted with such immediate satisfaction and unequivocal enthusiasm. I often have to remind myself that although most people love to eat - and everyone has to - few people consider reading one of life's basic necessities. Although I know perfectly well that this is the way things are, I am still disappointed that people in general turn first to my culinary concoctions and then, perhaps, to one of my books, if they have time and the mood suits.

Even for a lot of literate people books tend to be a subsidiary stimulus and comfort. As a teacher friend of mine in the Maritimes tells me, she goes down to the beach in front of her cottage late on a summer's afternoon taking some hors d'oeuvres, a cocktail and a good book with her. I feel sure that she lists these treats in the order of their importance to her and I have always suspected that, because she invariably has company on her beach excursions, she rarely gets around to opening the "good book".

So it is because of my way with food rather than words that I find myself assigned to a primitive hut, the smallest and least prepossessing of the erratically dispersed cabins alongside a fast-flowing western subarctic river. This camp caters to wealthy foreign fishermen who, according to the brochure, *enjoy incredible fishing and gourmet meals in a unique setting in the world's most scenic and pristine environment. Here salmon abound as nowhere else on earth and the food is out of this world.* No Canadians are booked in: I suppose they must consider the $8,000 (US) tab too steep for an eight day sojourn in a wilderness camp. Not only is our low dollar a deterrent, but even $8,000 Canadian is a lot of money, especially when most Canadians reckon they have rivers and woods galore within much easier reach than this one - and can visit them without paying a cent.

Although up to now I would have subscribed to this rationale, I am beginning to think that my well-to-do countrymen and women are missing out by not coming here. I've seen a lot of this country, coast to coast - north to south too - and never set eyes on anything quite so spectacular as this - or a river so chock-a-block with fish. Without this job, though, there's no way I would be here. Expensive vacations are well beyond my means.

Having just been ferried by helicopter from an outpost village some sixty miles north of here near the Yukon border, I stand outside the plywood shell which my son-in-law, the proprietor of this camp, allotted to me and I marvel at the view. From inside the hut none of this is visible. The door is solid, without glass or screen, and the only window is less than two feet square and too high up for me unless I stand on tiptoes. Besides, it looks out towards the encroaching forest and the outhouse at its edge, rather than the river.

Tonight is perhaps the only time I'll have to admire the

scenery. Tomorrow morning at dawn I expect to be in the cook-house preparing breakfast for early-rising fishermen.

These paying guests have not yet arrived. Besides me, in camp there are only my daughter Amy, who is to spell me off in the kitchen; Jason, her two-and-a-half-year old and my only grandson, who I am to keep an eye on during my time off and Amy's stint in the cookhouse; her husband Doug, the camp's owner; his hired seventeen-year-old helper Matt; and Mr. Dalton, the elderly father of one of the helicopter pilots, who is staying here free for a few days because Doug owes his pilot friend a favor.

The first three fishermen should be arriving in about an hour and the next contingent several hours after that. The two other clients, still in Whitehorse, will not get here until tomor-row morning. They will have to be driven the hundred or so miles to the outpost where the helicopters are parked and then airlifted down river. Because of the long, clear daylight hours in late June in this part of the world, Amy tells me that evening and early morning chopper charters pose no problems.

I walk toward the grassy knoll where Amy and Mr. Dalton are starting a bonfire. Amy remarks that, in years gone by, the clients have really enjoyed sitting around these evening fires, discussing their days' catches and toasting the sunset, if they have remembered to bring their own liquor supply. (Amy says that the only alcohol Doug brings in for the fishermen is wine and beer to accompany the evening meals.)

I think that, even if they do not much care for bonfires, late evening chitchats or sundowners, the clients would not want to spend a lot of time in their huts. Not if their accommodations are like mine. However I keep this thought to myself.

As I stand by, not feeling very conversational, Amy re-marks how the smoke deters the mosquitoes and flies which tend to appear in the waning daylight hours. She seems to have

forgotten temporarily how familiar I am with camping and coping with mosquitoes and black flies - though I can understand
why she feels like explaining: most of our camping was done
when Amy was about the age Jason is now. Amy's explanation
causes me to wonder how much of this summer's doings Jason
will remember.

While I watch, Amy lights the bark and twig tepee she
has built and Mr. Dalton positions several large poplar logs
nearby for when the small pieces are ablaze. I speculate about
how the fire will likely comfort these rich visitors who have
probably never been without electricity before. I imagine that
they will tell themselves that the fire will deter the grizzlies and
cougars, the full-time residents here, from venturing into camp.
At first, though, the visitors may forget that the fire will die
down soon after they retire. They probably won't realize either
that, once everything is quiet, the bears will feel free to conduct
an on site inspection.

Doug has told me casually that most years when he's
down here in June and early July a bear or two ventures into
camp from time to time. He easily distinguishes one grizzly from
another: according to Amy, he's even named the regulars.

I wonder if Doug has warned his clients about the grizzlies. I suspect not. Doug is not keen on communicating, especially with strangers. Even with family, he tends to steer clear
of explanations. Besides he doesn't think the bears are dangerous at this time of year: the salmon are so plentiful that he believes it would be hard to get the grizzlies worked up. Since
Doug is very knowledgeable about wildlife, I am inclined to
believe him.

As it is apparent that Amy and Mr. Dalton do not need
my help, I climb down over the bank and wander out across the
wide gravel bed to where Jason is fishing under Doug's super-
vision. Doug has deposited him in a plastic chair in the shal-

lows and, apparently, told him not to squirm. He must really have laid down the law because I have never seen Jason sit so still: he is motionless, transfixed by the fish swimming upriver in the eddies just beneath his feet and in the powerful current where his rod reaches. The salmon are flank to flank, bank to bank, and, it would appear, packed from surface to bottom of this clear, fast-flowing stream. I have never seen anything like this, even in pictures. It's surprising the *Geographic*'s photographers haven't been here. Small wonder that Jason is mesmerized.

I remind myself that, in the very remote past, the Miramichi, Saint John and Restigouche rivers in my home province must have produced such extraordinary bounty: more even than this relatively small tributary of the Taku, because the great New Brunswick rivers are so much wider and deeper than this one. Here the pebbly bottom is clearly visible and the opposite bank cannot be more than twenty feet away.

Since Doug runs his camp on catch-and-release principles, there is no pail full of the fish Jason has caught. While I watch, Jason, with Doug's help, reels in a big salmon. Doug carefully removes the hook and gently returns the fish to the water. Jason is being indoctrinated early with his father's methods.

Although I approve of Doug's behavior in this instance, I am too concerned about what seems to me Jason's precarious position to give my full consideration to fishing methods. I worry about Jason being swept away, but am afraid to let Doug know what I am thinking. I have learned the hard way that Doug has very little patience with other people's views - one of the reasons, I suspect, why he and Amy are having problems.

Anyway I can put these concerns on hold because the first guests are almost here. Jason and Doug have heard the chopper before I have. Jason is pointing up over the falls, and laughing.

In a single motion, Doug swings Jason, still in his chair, onto the gravel, and cautions him to stay where he is - out of reach of the helicopter which the pilot sets down neatly on the far stretch of gravel, just below the knoll where Amy and Mr. Dalton's fire is now burning brightly.

Jack, the pilot, after shutting down his machine, climbs out onto the gravel, signals casually to his passengers to disembark and saunters towards Doug and Jason and me. We walk towards him and, when we meet, he tells Doug that he won't be returning tonight because the second lot of clients has backed out.

"Some bastard told them this place wasn't worth coming to - had no electricity, no indoor plumbing, no bar. All that crap. So now those guys are off to a big, slick fish camp in Alaska. Place has all the frills, the bugger told them.

"Sorry 'bout that Doug," he remarks after a slight pause, not sounding particularly upset; then adds: "Anyhow, I'll bring in the last lot tomorrow morning. Since the guy's been here before, he must like it. We don't know anything, though, 'bout the gal he's got in tow this time, do we?"

Neither Jack nor Doug seems much concerned about the last minute cancellations. They aren't in any hurry either to cope with the newly-arrived fishermen who are standing near the helicopter looking lost.

Amy and Mr. Dalton get to the newcomers well before we do. I am relieved because I feel sure that Amy will save the day if anyone can. She is very good with people. Mr. Dalton is, I suspect, no slouch in that department either. He gives off first-rate vibes, seeming good-natured and reliable. Unflappable too, I'd guess.

But if, as I've gathered, this place has been going down hill these last few seasons I am not surprised. Amy hasn't been here since Jason was born, and I imagine she was the one who held things together. She is so eager to please - probably too eager for her own good, I sometimes think. It is Amy, not Doug, who has been invited to visit former clients and their families at their homes in Paris, Phoenix, Berlin and even as far away as Melbourne - though she has never been free to consider accepting any of these overtures.

Doug has admitted that he dislikes tourists, and it seems to me that this aversion must be apparent to the newcomers, even from a distance. Body language needs no translators. Small wonder Doug has got bookings for only one eight day session this season.

* * *

Although Amy has just met these would-be fishermen, she introduces them to Doug and Jason and me as if she has known them for some time. Since Jack has flown them down river, she assumes that he knows who they are, though he does not give the impression that this is so.

Doug has backed off and is standing too far away to make for comfortable introductions. It seems clear to me - and probably to the new arrivals - that he is well aware that he will get to know these strangers soon enough and doesn't want to act in a way which will hasten the inevitable exchanges.

From Amy's introductions we learn that Dr. Helmut Gunter is a German, a surgeon from Frankfurt; Pierre de Langley, a French wine-maker from Alsace-Lorraine; Ernesto Gomez, a Mexican rancher. My initial take is that none of these men seems representative of their nationalities, though I have to admit I haven't much to go on with either the German or the Mexican - only that they are certainly not the stereotypes an unsophisticated observer might expect.

Dr. Gunter does not look to have benefited from Hitler's supposedly ideal gene pool. He is only about two inches taller than I am, which would make him five foot six. Perhaps he looks more than that because his is a much heavier build than mine. He is flabby and pasty-faced. I would guess he is about fifty-five. Since he scarcely acknowledges Amy's introductions, my mother would have observed, if she were alive and here, that this man makes no attempt to put his best foot forward. I am not prepared for a European to be so lacking in social grace, but then I haven't spent much time in Europe. I think, though, that my compatriots in general, and myself in particular, expect Europeans to be more gracious and mannerly than we are.

Señor Gomez resembles none of his stereotypical countrymen in movies I've seen, nor does he look one bit like his handsome president, Vincente Fox, or the dapper and polished Mexican doctor I met years ago in Edinburgh. Ernesto Gomez, in fact, looks like a slob. His distended belly hangs over his none-too-clean jeans and from his hairy, exposed chest a thick gold chain dangles. He seems amiable, though, smiling and garrulous in not very idiomatic English. Some of his direct translations from Spanish are funny and he knows that this is so. He clearly enjoys playing the comedian. I find myself hoping he puts on lots of performances in the days to come: it looks to me as if the situation that's shaping up here will warrant considerable comic relief. Already he has made Amy, Mr. Dalton and me laugh out loud. Even Jason is laughing, responding, I suppose, to the Mexican's tone and gestures rather than his words. Pierre de Langley is smiling. Dr. Gunter is not.

Pierre de Langley is a tall and loose-limbed young man of about thirty and tentative in his movements. When, from a distance, I saw him unfold himself from the front seat of the helicopter and stumble as his feet reached the gravel, I was reminded of Mr. Hulot in the film, *Mr. Hulot's Holiday*. Since we are to be responsible for this man every day for the next eight days instead of merely watching his look-alike in a short comic flick, I find myself hoping that he will not turn out to be so accident-prone as Jacques Tati's depiction of the fictitious Mr. Hulot.

For the first time I give serious, though brief, consideration to the fact that we are a long way from help in an emergency. A helicopter wouldn't necessarily be available if Doug called for it on the spur of the moment on the two-way radio or satellite phone, and anyway there is no doctor in the village where the helicopters are stationed, just two outpost nurses. And, getting out to Whitehorse from the village would take considerably more time. Problems galore....

I scrub troublesome possibilities out of my mind and focus on the positive aspects of this Frenchman. He seems most eager to please, and I give him full marks when, in an obvious attempt to lighten Dr. Gunter's mood, he addresses the doctor in German, assuming perhaps that the doctor looks so glum because his knowledge of English is limited.

This assumption turns out to be incorrect: Dr. Gunter's English is fluent, though pedantic. He snubs Pierre de Langley's overture and scowls at Ernesto Gomez.

Shades of clashes to come, I fear, though I pretend not to notice that anything seems amiss. All the same, I feel relieved that I'll be spending my time in the kitchen rather than attempting to cope with what looks as if it may turn out to be a public relations crisis, with international implications. It crosses my mind now that Doug has perhaps witnessed similar standoffs in the ten years or so he has been in this business, so that his guarded - well, hostile is more like it - attitude may be somewhat understandable.

* * *

It is Matt who cheers everyone up. The lithe and sunny seventeen-year-old leaps down the bank, spouting apologies for not showing up sooner. He tells us that filling the shower tower with buckets of river water and distributing the wood he's split for the stoves in each cabin has taken him longer than he had anticipated.

He shoulders the three duffle bags, and staggers off towards the huts under what appears to be their considerable weight. It looks to me as if these visitors have brought heavier gear than Jack ordinarily allows each person to take aboard his chopper.

"Follow me, guys," Matt calls out to the three fishermen. "I'm supposed to be your fishing guide," I hear him explaining. Then, before he moves out of earshot, he adds, "But I do other stuff too. Just let me know if you need anything - more wood, water, whatever...."

Matt is a charmer; his appearance and takeover at this moment, a godsend.

Once I am alone in my hut I begin to worry about my ability to come up with the gourmet cuisine promised in the brochure. I face the fact that, although I concoct tasty meals, most of these would fall into the category of plain cooking. And although I have a few special dishes which at a stretch could pass for gourmet, I doubt I am the sort of chef these three foreign fishermen expect.

While I am stewing about my possible inadequacies in the kitchen, Amy and Jason knock on my door. I am surprised that Jason is still up and about: it's after ten. When Amy, her sister and brother were that age they went to bed at seven.

Amy reads my mind. "The light is so strong here late in the evening at this time of the year that it's hard for anyone to fall asleep early," she points out.

I nod, remembering the Inuit children I saw playing on

the Pangnirtung beach at midnight one summer years ago.

"We like to sleep in in the morning, though," Amy adds. This is my cue. I pick up on it. "Breakfast will be my responsibility. You know I love to get up early. Don't worry about the morning. Breakfasts are no big deal anyway. It's the rest of the meals that are worrying me," I confess.

But before Amy can respond I go on. "Tomorrow I'll make lunch too. At breakfast I'll ask one of the fishermen to catch and save a salmon. I'll make a chowder and salmon loaf. Everyone seems to love both these dishes. Not every single salmon has to be released, does it?"

"No, we use the odd one," Amy admits unenthusiastically. "The problem is that in the past I've found that, although the fishermen love to catch salmon, they don't want to eat them. You know, Mum," she reminds me, "how some of the folks back home think it's great to go out on the marshes picking mushrooms, even though they don't enjoy eating them."

I'm beginning to feel stressed. What am I going to do if my most successful meals don't meet with approval here?

"Well, suppose I bake a lasagna as a backup," I suggest. "You could make some of your wonderful sourdough biscuits to go with the chowder, salmon loaf and lasagna. It would be fun to tell your fishermen how you carry the fermented dough with you, just like the miners did during the gold rush. We can explain how this is fare unique to this part of the world. Give these visitors something to talk about when they get back to where they've come from..."

"Mum," Amy interrupts my monologue. "You've got to remember that these fishermen aren't like the Elderhostel group you were asked to give a talk to in the village the day Jack flew you down here. Mostly, they're not into learning. They don't want to attend lectures - and we just don't get anyone here who's on a shoestring."

Then she changes the subject. "Now about dinner to-night," Amy says in a take charge kind of voice, which I don't associate with this dreamy and delicate daughter of mine but which nevertheless sounds vaguely familiar, "I'll make a Greek salad to go with the beef Stroganoff we planned. For dessert that rum and date cake you said you'd make after lunch is always a marvelous treat."

I ponder this newly authoritative voice, still wondering where she's come by it - and realize with a shock that she is sounding like me planning similar moves on my home turf. Funny thing. Our roles seem to have been reversed. I tell myself that this turnabout is going to take some getting used to. I can't think of anything to say, so I merely nod.

Amy continues to tell me what's what. I begin to see that she is a pro at managing a woods kitchen; that she's confronted all the difficulties and found ways around them.

"Without a fridge we have to remember to use the salad things and fresh vegetables before they rot - and the meat before it thaws too much and spoils. The coolers will keep the turkey and ham semi-frozen till the third and fourth days. And the day after we've cooked the turkey you can make one of your fabulous stir-fries, Mum."

Amy thinks my attention has begun to wander - which is true - so she stresses the *Mum*.

*   *   *

Daylight comes early. There have been very few dark hours. It's chilly, though, this morning. Very chilly indeed. I light the camp stove in my hut and crawl back into my sleeping bag while I go over what I need to do as soon as I get dressed.

I figure that lighting the stove in the dining tent will be

my first priority. Then I'll make coffee.

The thought of the freshly-brewed coffee gets me out of bed - that and worrying that one of the clients will materialize at the cookhouse before I do. Surprisingly, in the few minutes my stove has been going it has warmed the hut enough for not too uncomfortable dressing. As I pull on my jeans and sweatshirt I wonder idly whether the clients will know how to manage their stoves. Well, that's not my worry, I tell myself. Matt's department probably.

Dr. Gunter turns up shortly after I've lit the stove in the dining tent, set the table there and made coffee. He nods formally and politely, and says that, yes, he would like coffee.

Just as I am taking his breakfast order - French toast and sausages - Matt breezes in. Dr. Gunter responds quite warmly to Matt's greeting. He even smiles - sort of.

Matt tells the doctor that French toast is his favorite breakfast and he's a pro at making it. "I'll make your toast," he volunteers, "while Amy's mother does the sausages. Get you coffee first, though. How's that?"

"Very good indeed," Herr Gunter says, directing quite a generous smile at Matt this time.

I suggest to Matt that he have breakfast with Dr. Gunter and I hand over to him a jug of pure New Brunswick maple syrup I've brought with me - for pancakes really, but which will, I'm sure, jazz up the French toast too. "The doctor probably doesn't know about how special maple syrup is," I warn Matt. "So you'd better tell him about it."

"Geez, I don't know anything about that stuff either," Matt laughs, "so you'd better tell him."

I do as Matt suggests, but although Dr. Gunter listens politely to my explanation, it is clear that he is not used to giving servants the time of day. Because I am presiding over the kitchen just now, he has labeled me as a servant - an old one too

- surely not his social or intellectual equal, and no 'bunny' either. Not even in the same snack bracket as Matt who he reckons is an authority on fishing.

Besides, Matt is young and handsome, promising too, Dr. Gunter probably thinks. Suddenly I see Matt as I imagine he appears to Dr. Gunter - an ideal Germanic type, blue-eyed, flaxen-haired, upright, athletic, responsive and responsible, rather like the young German Michael York portrayed in *Cabaret*, though younger.

Over breakfast Matt and Dr. Gunter talk about fishing. Matt is laying out plans for the day. Dr. Gunter seems pleased. He nods from time to time as Matt explains.

As I clear away the breakfast dishes, Matt looks up smiling and tells me how much he loves the maple syrup. "Just think of what I've been missing all these years," he quips.

Dr. Gunter nods and smiles at Matt.

"Very nice," he remarks.

Does he mean the maple syrup or Matt? I wonder. Probably both.

*   *   *

Our other two fishermen appear together. Pierre de Langley says he will have an English breakfast.

Although I find this odd, I try not to bat an eye.

"Fried bread, tomatoes, sausages, fried eggs, marmalade - and TEA?" I ask, secretly convinced he has made a mistake - and should be ordering croissants and coffee.

He nods. "Please. Everything for an English breakfast."

"And you?" I ask Señor Gomez.

"Same as them both," he says laughing, nodding toward the other two fishermen and rubbing his belly. "I got lots of room here."

Dr. Gunter gets up to leave and Matt says he'll take him to a good fishing spot in about half an hour.

Since Amy, Doug, Jason and Mr. Dalton all turn up before I've finished coping with Pierre de Langley and Ernesto Gomez, I am rushed during the next hour. But I manage pretty well I think for a newcomer to the catering business.

Pierre de Langley asks where we bought the peach conserve - the closest I could come to marmalade - and I tell him I made it at home and brought it with me.

"Ah, I must get your recipe then, Madame, if that is possible," he says. "Cooking and fishing are my two passions. Well, perhaps art too. I wish to be able to paint, but that is another subject.... That peach conserve - is that what you called it, yes? - is gourmet. I could eat it every day."

I interrupt the Frenchman's eulogy to tell him that I will indeed give him the recipe - and, in an effort to please him further, point out that Amy is a first-rate watercolor artist who has sold her paintings all over the world. "Perhaps she'll give you a lesson or two," I suggest.

When I glance at Amy I realize at once that she is not pleased by my suggestion. Like Amy herself, I tend to be too eager to please guests, forgetting sometimes the extent of the ensuing obligations. Still I am, I remind myself, old enough to know better than to volunteer someone else's time and expertise. I am beginning to stress Amy and I am sorry. I rationalize that it was the Frenchman's use of *gourmet* which set me off, making me suddenly silly and overconfident.

I return to the kitchen to wash dishes and, before I am well under way, Mr. Dalton turns up to help me. He says he likes doing dishes. Although I have trouble believing him, I am delighted with his attitude - and help. I can't even pretend that I enjoy dishwashing. At home I am wedded to my dishwasher. Still, I have to admit that Mr. Dalton's presence makes coping with the dishes not unpleasant.

As soon as the kitchen is set to rights, I begin preparations for lunch. Matt brings me a salmon which Dr. Gunter has caught.

* * *

When lunch is ready, keeping warm in the oven, and I am playing with Jason on the gravel near the river, Jack lands the helicopter bearing the last two paying guests. Jason abandons the fort we are constructing and heads off toward the helicopter. I catch him up, aware that I must keep him away from the still rotating blades. It does not seem as if Jack is going to shut his machine down this time - just drop off his passengers and leave.

The newcomers are Billy Joe Latimer, an obese fifty-year-old, and a skinny girl called Cathy Jacobs, who looks half his age, or less. Both are from Arizona. He owns a car dealership: she is a nurse. Although they have arrived together and are to share the same cabin, they do not appear to like one another. I wonder why. The girl's hostility is almost tangible. The man seems apathetic. Spaced out.

Well, he seems apathetic until I mention that lunch is ready. He wants to know what we're having - and says he likes lasagna. Cathy does not seem interested in eating. She looks around and does not appear impressed with what she sees. I'd bet my bottom dollar that fishing bores her and that she expected a posher setup than this one. I suspect Jack has come to the same conclusion about Billy Joe and Cathy as I have and has decided to lift himself out of camp before Cathy and Billy Joe decide they want to leave. Once he's gone, their only choice, barring emergencies, is to stay put. Neither looks up to opting for an uncharted sixty mile hike through bogs and over mountains to get to the only village for miles around.

Lunch seems to me the best way to keep them here - and this turns out to be so. All the clients chow down. Salmon loaf, chowder, lasagna, coleslaw, sourdough biscuits, chocolate chip cookies vanish. Pierre de Langley asks for the recipe for the cookies, which he finds delectable and exotic. He tells me he has had uninspiring biscuits on visits to England and tasty pastries throughout Europe, but no chocolate chip cookies anywhere. Amazing!

But it is the lasagna which has posed problems. Not because it's not good enough for these supposedly discerning palates, but because our guests find it too good. There hasn't been enough to go around. Although I made four deep, wide dishes, none was left for Doug, Amy or me. Although all our visiting menfolk had multiple helpings, Ernesto and Billy Joe didn't know when to stop. They seemed to be engaged in a who-can-eat-the-most-fastest contest.

Now that the table has been cleared, they shift their behinds restlessly on the wooden benches. Ernesto gets up first, belches, guffaws and announces, "Siesta time."

"Good idea," Billy Joe agrees. "Come on Cathy."

Cathy stalls. "I need to check out some of the menus with Amy and her mum. You know there's things you're not supposed to eat. Your folks expect me to pay attention to your food. After all, that's why I'm here," she adds pointedly, raising her voice and looking around the table, obviously trying to make the point that she and Billy Joe are not the usual kind of item - whatever that might be.

But only Dr. Gunter and I are attending to Cathy. Amy has followed Jason outside and Pierre de Langley is stumbling along in their wake. Since I am standing at the entrance to the dining tent, I hear him tell Amy that Jason is the most perfect child he has ever seen. "He resembles to his mother," he adds quietly.

Matt is shifting his weight from one sneaker to the other, eyes glued to Dr. Gunter, waiting to see if he intends to fish after lunch. But the doctor is watching Cathy with what I take to be considerable interest.

"You like to fish?" he inquires.

"Depends," she replies bluntly, looking him over. "Why?"

"Well, Matt will, I think, show me another good spot on the river early this afternoon. You might like to come along ... since Billy Joe will sleep just now. It will be pleasant."

"Not a bad idea, I suppose," Cathy says gracelessly. "Okay.... Just wait a couple minutes, will you, till I talk to Amy." This is not a question. Cathy is delivering an ultimatum.

Dr. Gunter beams at her. I wonder what he sees in her.

* * *

The next few days pass quite successfully, considering the disparate natures of the clientele and the lack of facilities they'd probably expected. It seems I needn't have worried about the meals. They have been hugely successful.

Cathy spends a lot of time with the doctor and Amy too, when she can collar my busy daughter. Amy tells me that Cathy has confided in her that Billy Joe has a serious drug habit as well as an eating disorder, and that she's been hired by his affluent and straight-laced parents to curb his various excesses.

"It's one helluva dumbass job," she's told Amy. "Just watch me make tracks when we get back home. No way anyone can cope with that son of a bitch."

Amy thinks Cathy is right. "I sure wouldn't want to be in her shoes right now," Amy tells me, and I have to agree.

No one except Ernesto wants to spend time with Billy

Joe. But what is surprising is that Ernesto gives every indication that he genuinely enjoys Billy Joe's company - and not just because of their mutual rivalry in outdoing one another at mealtimes.

Even more surprising is that Billy Joe is beginning to respond positively to this friendly attention. I guess that being liked is a new experience for him. And although he is clearly hesitant about counting on Ernesto's camaraderie lasting, he is obviously enjoying the Mexican's comicality and apparent concern for his well-being. He laughs out loud at Ernesto's irreverent comments and relaxes visibly in the jovial company of his newfound friend.

Tonight the two gluttons have stayed behind in the meal tent to finish off what's left of the bottles of wine, together with the remaining crackers, cheese, smoked salmon and olives which they have transferred from the nearby serving table. They are doubled up over something Ernesto has said when Billy Joe spots Cathy walking by, deep in conversation with the doctor.

I have just come back to the meal tent to clear the table, so I overhear bits of both conversations.

Cathy is telling Dr. Gunter about killing rattlers on her way to school in rural Arizona. I pretty much know what she's going to say because she's already given this spiel to Amy and me in the kitchen, a monologue provoked by my asking, 'Don't you worry about snakes down there?' It is clear, though, that she has hooked Dr. Gunter, that he thinks she's got bags of guts, which I expect is true.

As I start to remove the dishes, I realize that Billy Joe is no longer attending to Ernesto. He is scowling into the space which Cathy and the doctor occupied a moment earlier. Ernesto, unwilling to lose his most receptive listener, is not about to let the poison fester in his newfound friend's brain.

"Hey man," he says to Billy Joe, resting his meaty hand

on the other's fat wrist, "that one's not your kind of gal.... Mine neither." He laughs. "Too flat and skinny. No sense of humor neither.

"Women! A problem anyway my friend. Who's to tell what makes them clock."

"Tick," Billy Joe corrects automatically.

"Yeh, well tick.... Anyhow, don't take them so serious. I don't or I'd be a wreck. I get and lose chicks so fast you'd think I'd be the most depressed guy 'round. But what you say in English, 'Variety is the chili of life?'"

"Spice, not chili," Billy Joe interrupts.

Ernesto, seemingly unaware of the intrusion, plunges on. "I pay three ex-wives and their kids - my kids. All boys. All look like me. Good looking, eh? So you see, everything works out good. Lots more babes out there for rich and handsome guys like me and you.... No?"

He slaps Billy Joe on the back and laughs, but doesn't wait for a reply. "You know I got lots of experience and I tell you it feels real good to be between wives and girlfriends like just now. Have fun with your freedom while you got it, I say.

"All my wives loved my dough. Still do. Me, they say I'm a jerk. Hard to believe, eh?" Ernesto bangs the table with his fist, presumably to emphasize his point of view - and guffaws.

"Lighten up man. You got to enjoy what you got - and be thankful for what you don't got."

Billy Joe tries to smile at this tidbit of garbled logic, but doesn't say anything. Ernesto doesn't give him a chance to squeeze a word in edgeways anyway.

"Now, tell me 'bout yourself, man. Must be something turns you on 'cept grub, gals and cars.... Not fishing, I'll bet.... I don't see you running down there (he gestures vaguely towards the river) to spend a lot of time pulling fishes out and throwing them back again. So tell me what REALLY makes you clock."

Ernesto leans closer to Billy Joe. "Now you just tell me."

"Knives," Billy Joe whispers.

"Knives, guns, sure. You and me, we're real macho men, so naturally we go for knives. But what, I mean, you like to think about? You know, MAKE."

"I MAKE knives," Billy Joe articulates clearly. Then he starts to shout. "But the goddam customs man confiscated the ones I brought with me when we came across the border.... Had to buy all new stuff in Vancouver. What d'they think? That I'm some kind of crazy terrorist? Shit! Makes me madder 'n hell."

Ernesto seems really interested and impressed. "Knives," he repeats, savoring the word. "Well, I'd sure like to see your knives. The new ones you're working on."

Billy Joe appears gratified.

I leave the meal tent, thinking I'll finish clearing up later in the afternoon. I am anxious to retire to my hut for a brief rest while Jason is having his nap and the camp seems at least temporarily peaceful. I walk by the picnic table where Amy is giving Pierre de Langley a painting lesson and then past the slow alder fire Doug is building to smoke salmon.

* * *

I wake up suddenly wondering where I am and then quickly recall the circumstances. I remember that when I'd lain down I hadn't meant to drift off. Briefly I lie still, listening for sounds of activity and hearing nothing. Smoke from Doug's fire filters through the window. I cough. Perhaps the smoke has wakened me. I consult my watch. My snooze has lasted less than half an hour. Not to worry, I tell myself. I'm not late for anything.

When I emerge from my hut I decide to head for the

river, thinking I'll wade in the shallows and enjoy the peace and quiet there for a few minutes before Jason wakes up. But as I step out from behind the cookhouse I am face to face with a sight so bizarre that I can't believe I'm awake and in the midst of a scene straight out of anyone's worst nightmare.

The formerly peaceful knoll above the gravel and river has been transformed into what looks like the set of a horror movie - except that no one is moving or saying anything. Amazed and appalled by what I see, I am gripped by the paralysis which seems to have brought everyone else to a standstill: the nightmarish feeling of not being able to move.

Cathy is pinned to the poplar tree at the edge of the bank by what looks like a jade-handled knife. There is no blood, so I assume the knife has gone through her sweatshirt, not her arm.

Billy Joe is leaning against the cookhouse, seemingly poised to let fly at Cathy with another knife. Whether he intends to kill her or just scare her is unclear.

Doug, who is standing in the open on the opposite side of the cookhouse to me, has his bear gun trained on Billy Joe. He looks ready to use it. I hope Billy Joe realizes that, although Doug would be very reluctant to shoot a grizzly - even if the bear seemed a threat - he wouldn't hesitate to fire on a human being who was stupidly endangering others' safety. I get the feeling, though, that Billy Joe isn't capable just now of reacting rationally. He looks as if he doesn't care about anything. Sort of crazed. Maybe he's been doing drugs again. Who knows? I am surprised my brain isn't as incapacitated as my body. Again like a nightmare.

Amy and Pierre de Langley are still at the picnic table, pencils, paints and sketch pads spread out between them. Amy is facing the ugly scene. Her face has the pallor of a patient slowly emerging from an anaesthetic. Her expression says, *this just can't be happening* - which is what I am thinking too. The

Frenchman has his back to this macabre still life, and I suspect Amy has warned him to hold still, not to turn around.

I look over my shoulder to make sure that I am actually where I seem to be, that I am not dreaming, that the hut is behind me, just where it was when I stepped out. But what I see behind me is even more horrifying than the scene before me. Hard to believe, but it is so. Jason has escaped from his cot, opened the door in Doug and Amy's shanty and is running towards me.

I do not know what to do. The least motion on my part might trigger a worse situation than the existing one. Besides I still seem to be incapable of action.

Jason stops when he sees everyone so strangely posed. Then he takes a few steps towards Cathy. I think it is the knife with the beautiful green handle that he wants to see close up. But before he can reach the poplar Cathy is pinned to, he stops and points down towards the gravel. He has seen something the rest of us haven't, something obscured by the leaves on the poplar. Where Jason is looking there are no leaves.

"Aggie," he burbles, sounding delighted. "Twins," he adds, laughing.

Doug and Amy are no longer focused on Billy Joe and Cathy. Doug moves forward more quickly than I would have thought possible and scoops Jason up. He backs up slowly towards my side of the cookhouse, Jason under one arm, gun tucked under the other. As he hands Jason to me and repositions the gun, a massive grizzly and her two cubs amble into the clearing, bypassing Cathy without seeming to notice her.

"Jesus," Billy Joe mutters, backing around the far corner of the cookhouse, looking as if he wishes he could disappear altogether.

Cathy looks whiter than ever, but remains motionless, pinned helplessly to the tree.

Jason is still chortling. "Aggie... twins," he says again, pointing as if we can't see for ourselves.

Now that I feel responsible for the youngster in my arms I am less addled, the paralysis beginning to ebb. I remember that Doug has named the bears which frequent this part of the river. So this is Agnes, the bear Doug says comes into camp now and then to show off her current offspring.

"No one move," Doug orders in a firm, quiet voice. Since he is standing in front of Jason and me, I figure we are in a safer position than anyone else. I am most worried about Amy in her exposed position.

We all hold still while Agnes and her babies wander around the clearing. They circle the picnic table so that Pierre de Langley has his first view of the grizzly and her cubs. He falls backward in what looks like a dead faint.

The Frenchman's fall apparently surprises the mother bear. She stops and stares at the inert form, then, with a shrug proceeds with her tour, much, I imagine, as she might if a tree had suddenly fallen near her path on one of her forest excursions.

She swings past Dr. Gunter and Matt who have just reached the clearing, but does not glance in their direction. Then she heads back over the bank and down towards the river, her youngsters close behind her.

* * *

For the last few days of their stay, the clients are models of good behavior - considerate of one another, thankful, I am sure, to be alive and unharmed. But there is something more to their new attitudes. Having been within arm's length of one of the world's most awe-inspiring creatures in her pristine natural environment has moved them, seemingly making each less egotistical, less set in their ways.

One by one they express a wish to visit the decaying grave house on the other side of the river, above the falls. To everyone's surprise, Dr. Gunter says he can understand why the Tlingit shaman, whose 'house' it is, would want to be interred there. "I will never come to rest in such a place," he observes thoughtfully, sadly. "Money will not buy a spot like this."

The others nod and Doug, who once told me that he would like this grave house to be his final resting place, no longer seems to view this crop of clients with such distaste.

THE WHALER

Selling the Boston Whaler to help pay the medical expenses turned out to be less of a sacrifice than we would have expected. It was in fact something of a blessing, though neither of us was willing to concede that at the time.

The Whaler was part of a dream, and dismantling a dream tends to be more traumatic than making more practical adjustments. With the Whaler we imagined we could reach our island farm under our own steam. (The farm, by the way, is another romantic investment, since it is really just fifty acres of sand, swamp, scrub poplar, pin cherry, mountain ash and alder.)

To get on or off the island without owning a vessel we have to take the government-subsidized fishing boat which crosses the Strait on Tuesdays, Thursdays and Fridays at dawn and comes back in the late afternoon. It's only fifty cents each way. Fifty cents for nine miles - sometimes nine rough or foggy miles - is not a bad bargain these days.

In the four years we owned the Whaler we never did get her as far as the island. We never even managed to get her across the lake - a former mill pond - and back without a lot of trouble.

So what that the Whaler had the much-touted double

fiberglass hull and Archie's boat is an old-fashioned single-hulled wooden fishing boat! Archie's boat is reliable and the Whaler wasn't - at least not under our management.

Gordon said more than once in exasperation that he thought everything on the Whaler was connected backwards - though neither of us knew enough about motors, circuits and lights to make an accurate assessment. A friend of ours, though, who's a mechanical/electrical whiz did back Gordon up on this as far as the trailer connections were concerned. It took him every evening for three weeks to trace down all the wires and connect them properly, so that the signal lights would flash on the correct sides, instead of the left signal operating the right light and vice versa.

Part of the trouble was that, when the old wires had frayed, the original owner had simply added new ones alongside them. You've never seen such a maze of wires - about the number you'd expect to find linking the gauges on *Discovery* or *Challenger*.

We bought the Whaler secondhand from a man called James Thomas on the South Shore. He said he'd had it for fifteen years, that he'd bought it new in Boston when he'd worked there. During the time he'd owned it, he explained, he had replaced the original console and seats with innovations of his own and had tinkered with all the mechanisms - motor, fuel line, lights, C-Bee.

Maybe he only said everything worked. After all, he never showed us. He did say when we left that he was "real sorry to let her go - so cheap too." These parting words were clearly meant as a delicate reminder that, at $10,000 for everything, we had gotten a bargain. He knew that we knew that brand new Whalers cost roughly $1,000 a foot - they're probably more now, everything is - and that didn't include a motor. Mr. Thomas had, as he told us magnanimously at the beginning of our negotiations, "just thrown in the motor for free." I wonder if he'd conned us. He sounded genuine, though. We liked Mr. Thomas.

It was winter when we bought the Whaler, and she was high and dry in Mr. Thomas's barn - riding above undulating masses of sweet-smelling hay. We were impressed at the time with how clean she looked - as if she hadn't been near the water or exposed to the elements in her life. We had to agree with Mr. Thomas that she didn't look her age.

We tried the Whaler out for the first time just after the lake ice broke up. Spring was early that year. The sun was strong for April, and water from the Joe Brook and the surrounding hills had covered the ice with a foot or more of water. Then the wind had finished the job, cracking the sodden mass and sweeping grey cakes down towards the bridge.

"We'll take a spin across the lake and back," Gordon had announced enthusiastically. "It's a great day, and we won't be out there long enough to get cold. No need for a jacket. Fifteen minutes will do it. This lake's really too small for such a big, powerful boat, but I have to try her out here before putting her in at the shore."

It seemed like a good idea.

We were across the lake in jig time. A twenty foot Whaler with a seventy horsepower engine on a mill pond - a quarter-of-a-mile-across pond, boosted a few years ago to lake status by the suburbanites who moved into Fred Lumsden's carrot field at the north end when he retired and sold up - is about like having one of those children's wind-up boats on the bathtub. You no sooner put it in the water than it's bumping the edge.

The right sort of boat for the pond - Lumsden's Pond was the old name, Silver Lake the new one - is a canoe or a small sailing dingy like the one the children learned on. If you have to have a motorboat, the aluminum boat with the seven-

and-a-half horsepower motor we bought secondhand twenty
years ago from the local jeweller is just the thing. It putts over
to our woodlot and back again, hauling a small boom.

Gordon, used to this seven-and-a-half horsepower engine, appeared to panic as we neared the shore at what seemed
like a wild speed. It *was* a wild speed. I was terrified. It looked
as if we were going to run right up into John Hirshfield's woods.

The Whaler seemed to be going too fast to turn without
spilling us into the water. At the last moment, Gordon did what
I would have done under the circumstances if I'd been at the
wheel and had had the wit. He cut the motor.

What a relief! Peace and quiet flooded in. There we sat,
all in one piece, bobbing gently about fifteen feet from shore.
The spring sunshine poured down. No one was near. The firs
and spruces in this sheltered cove grow close to the water. It
was too early in the season for the birches and maples interspersed among them to be showing new green. Even so, everything looked fresh and new. I always feel liberated just after the
ice goes out. It was an idyllic moment.

Gordon quickly recovered his equilibrium. He looked
distinctly pleased with himself. He'd gotten the monster motor
going and gotten it stopped again, his look said, and now, with a
little more practice, he'd have it tamed. Then we would be able
to zoom along the coast as easily as the mounties and the coast-
guard did in their Whalers.

"Well, that was good, wasn't it?" he said. "It works. I
guess we'd better head back now. I said we'd only be out fifteen
minutes, and I want to keep my word. It won't even be that."

Now Gordon knows I think he is never reliable about
time. It's true. He goes downtown to get vinegar for the relish
that's been through the chopper and is all ready for the final
stage, or to get a gas fill-up, and he comes back hours later. He
doesn't even realize he's been gone long. He's chatted with this

person and that, and he doesn't seem to believe me if I tell him I've been waiting hours. So now he was underlining the fact that, this time anyway, he was going to keep his word - was, in fact, going to do better than he had promised.

The motor wouldn't start again. Gordon tried to get it going, but it didn't show even a flicker of life. Starting it up seemed as hopeless a proposition as getting a car motor going without booster cables when you've left the lights on all night. The cove, with no one else in sight, seemed much less alluring all of a sudden.

"Well," said Gordon, "there's nothing for it. We'll have to pull her back along the shore."

I had forgotten that a big boat like the Whaler does not come equipped with oars. It's obviously too wide and heavy to row. So here we were, only a quarter mile from home in a straight line, but with no way of getting there directly. Our only option was to walk around the shoreline in the shallows. That way it's about five miles. It was the longest five miles I ever remember. Walking in a few feet of water is no great shakes at the best of times, unless you're wading a very short distance for fun in mid-summer and the bottom is even and sandy. Alternately pulling and pushing a twenty foot boat as you inch forward doesn't help. The pond bottom is rocky in some places, muddy in others, and the water hadn't warmed up yet. We had to keep climbing out onto the shore to get rid of the numbness in our feet and legs.

*   *   *

We didn't take the Whaler out again until mid-July. The mechanic took a long time to repair whatever was broken. I think Gordon said some sort of pin had sheared off. This was a problem apparently because the motor was so old that the manu-facturers had stopped producing anything similar. The repairman said he'd had to make a piece to fit.

When we were ready to launch the boat again, Gordon asked along a friend who was supposed to be an old hand with power boats, and it was on this friend's advice that we put the Whaler in on a tidal river about a mile from where it empties into the sea. The afternoon was beautiful - sunny, calm and still. "A perfect day!" Doug, Gordon's friend, announced.

Gordon and Doug settled me in the stern where they made it clear that, like a child in bygone times, I was *to be seen and not heard.* I would like to have asked if all the weeds exposed by the receding tide weren't going to be a problem. I didn't though. Doug had told Gordon he'd put his boat in here every summer when he'd had a cottage a couple of miles down the coast.

Gordon was convinced that Doug knew what he was talking about. And indeed Doug radiated such an air of common sense, evenness and amiability that you wanted to believe in him.

The motor started at once and we moved slowly down the channel with the ebbing tide. Gordon went as slow as he could. "Good old boy," I said to myself.

Doug wasn't saying anything. He brought out his pipe, filled it carefully from his leather pouch, lighted it up and settled back, puffing comfortably. Amphora perfumed the air. It's an aroma I like (out of doors) but Gordon hates. I like it so much, in fact, I always reckoned that if I ever took up smoking I'd get a pipe and smoke amphora. Gordon didn't complain, though. He was obviously too relieved to have Doug along - a sort of insurance policy if anything went wrong.

Doug wasn't the only safeguard against possible disaster either. Gordon had brought along the ancient seven-and-a-half horsepower motor. Screwed onto the stern alongside its seventy horse-powered relative, it looked ridiculous - but nonetheless comforting.

We passed out of the river into the Strait. The salt water was clear. We had left the weeds behind in the river. We seemed to be fine. I settled back and looked around. Seabirds wheeled in the distance, and on the horizon there were other boats. I'd never seen the sea so calm.

Then all at once the motor stopped. There was no warning, no cough or splutter.

I felt sorry for Gordon. But at least, I comforted myself, Doug was here. He'd know what to do.

Doug didn't move though. He didn't say anything either. He just kept on puffing. He smiled and nodded to me. Gordon broke out in a lather. It had dawned on him, I could tell, that Doug hadn't the vaguest idea about what to do next.

I tried to hail a speedboat which had come in close enough to have a look at us - but the man and two women just waved back and grinned. I guess they thought we were stopped on purpose - to fish maybe - and that I was just being friendly.

Gordon was furious, but trying to conceal his anger because of Doug. The sweat poured down his forehead. He always perspires like that when he's ready to let go.

Still, he didn't lose his temper as he might have if there'd been no one else except me in the boat. "Well," he announced grimly, "we'd better take her back on the auxiliary." (I almost smiled, thinking of that tiny motor as an auxiliary for such a boat as the Whaler. But I didn't dare.) Gordon paused, and then, sounding defeated, remarked: "I don't know what else to do." He turned to Doug.

Doug nodded and puffed. "Good idea."

The small motor was our salvation. It had never failed before on our slow-motion trips around the pond, and it didn't fail us now. It propelled the Whaler back into the river and almost to the landing place before it started to choke and splutter.

"Those damn weeds," Gordon muttered. He cut the motor and jumped into the water, which was only chest deep and warm. He pulled us in to shore and up onto the ramp.

*   *   *

We didn't use the Whaler again that year - or the next. Whatever had happened to the motor in the river or on the Strait had been terminal. The mechanic said there was nothing he could do this time. "She was all seized up."

We couldn't afford a new motor - and we didn't even contemplate another secondhand one. What held us back too was the realization that one new motor was not enough. We needed two. It wasn't hard to imagine what might happen on our way to the island if our single engine conked out four or five miles at sea.

When we did get the new motors - one seventy and a thirty-five as the auxiliary - I didn't really want to go along for the trial run. My hip was hurting, and, although I didn't want to admit the fact, even to myself, I'd had enough of the Whaler. "Why," I suggested, "don't you and Doug take the boat out this time? I'll stay at home with Abby and Inkermann. They have only one more day at home."

But Gordon was adamant. He absolutely insisted that we all go along. Abby was enthusiastic. She loved boats. Her only concern was Inkermann. He hated boats.

We both remembered how touchy he'd been about getting onto fishing boats when I was researching the first island book. The fishermen who agreed to take us out to their islands had all been keen on taking him along. "A real fisherman's dog, a Lab is," one old fisherman had told us enthusiastically. "Great dogs! No trouble."

But, although Inkermann loved water, he was uneasy on

boats. He froze at the very sight, and in this rigid state had to be lifted aboard. He was too well brought up to complain, but his dislike of the experience was manifest in his utter dejection the entire time he was on board. The rougher the trip, the more he trembled. Just watching him was enough to convince anyone that - with the sort of special foresight often attributed to animals - he anticipated an imminent descent into the briny depths.

Gordon had never seen Inkermann's reaction to boats: Gordon had never been islanding with Abby and Inkermann and me. Ordinarily Inkermann was so amiable, so even-tempered and enthusiastic about being taken places, that it was hard to imagine that he could undergo an entire personality change when faced with an excursion by boat.

So Gordon insisted and we all went along. This time we launched the Whaler at the yacht club. There was a good wide ramp and we had no difficulties putting the boat in. The only problem was getting Inkermann in. Lifting a stiff and trembling seventy-five pound Lab into a boat is no easy operation. Besides, it looks silly. Gordon was embarrassed.

He has often make cracks about how ridiculous people look carrying miniature poodles or Pomeranians. He never imagined that he would ever end up with any dog - let alone a full-sized Labrador retriever, that most athletic of canines and fitting companion for the most macho man - in his arms.

He soon had an audience. A couple came over to the side of their yacht to get a better view. They acted as if they hadn't seen such a funny performance for a long time. The man grinned till his face must have ached, and the woman laughed out loud. Gordon's neck reddened.

Not an auspicious start!

Still, we had no other difficulties in the harbor. The motor started at once, and we churned sedately past the yacht and its no longer visible occupants. Once outside, the Whaler was everything the ads said it should be. We skimmed easily along the coast. The new motor ate the miles. There was not a single hitch.

Nevertheless, Gordon was careful not to lose sight of the coastline. He was doubtless thinking that if the motor cut out, chances were we'd gradually drift ashore. There was a gentle onshore breeze. Conditions were perfect.

Gradually Gordon relaxed and offered us each a turn at the wheel. "Nothing to it," he shouted above the motor. Abby and I took our turns. It was true: there was nothing to it.

We must have gone about forty or fifty miles before we turned back. We had just passed the Buctouche light. Now the breeze was against us and stiffening, as they used to say in the nautical yarns I read as a child.

The Whaler cut through each new-made wave determinedly and did not falter. That was not the problem. The trouble was that the spray from each wave blew over the top of the console glass and landed on Abby and Inkermann and me in the stern. In short order we were soaked and shivering - Inkermann from fear rather than chill, because it's hard, impossible maybe, to get a Labrador too wet and cold if he's happy with the circumstances.

Gordon did not know that we were drenched and miserable and jounced unmercifully on the unpadded seats every time the boat slapped a wave. If he had, there was not much he could have done about it. As it was, he sat dry behind the glass which protected him and bounced lightly on the well-sprung, foam-cushioned chair.

The relaxed cast of his shoulders stated that he was enjoying being in control. He seemed mesmerized too by the hum of the motor and the rhythmic thudding of the waves.

I vowed that, if I lived through this misery, I'd never go on a boat again - well, not a pleasure craft anyway. What a misnomer! Pleasure craft!

After what seemed like hours - was in fact hours, since the outgoing tide, combined with the freshening wind, contrived to hold us back as we neared the harbor - we approached the entrance. The motor labored. Gordon's shoulders tensed. He was convinced, I'm sure, that something was wrong with the engine. He had not taken into account the conjunction of tide and wind with the river's current pushing against us.

We made the harbor though. I was almost in tears and Inkermann was whining, doubtless smelling the proximity of land and hoping for release from this nasty situation. Abby, more stoical than either Inkermann or me, was silent and white and ill-looking. The lights had gone out of her warm, brown eyes, which now looked like *burnt holes in a blanket* - my mother's favorite expression for my eyes when she knew that I was coming down with something as a child.

Gordon turned around now to see how we were enjoying ourselves. Clearly he was amazed at how soaked and miserable we looked. Concerned and addled, he cut the motor. His panicked look said, *Better get the whole crew ashore before one of them's done for.*

He started the motor up again, but he must, in his haste, have shifted into reverse. The boat started backwards for the breakwater. Gordon fiddled with the gears. They seemed locked. He turned the wheel full round, steering the Whaler away from the rocks, and headed for the ramp - backwards.

People who'd been on the wharf when we entered the harbor had now stopped whatever they'd been doing and hurried to the edge where they stood looking down at us open-mouthed. Gordon carried on backwards. It was clear that he no longer cared how ridiculous his performance might look. He was going to get that Whaler onto the ramp quickly any way he could.

*   *   *

That was the last time we used the Whaler. It sat in the back yard under a tarp for ages, and finally one August day a few months before my operation a Cape Bretoner showed up in response to our advertisement and bought the boat. He thought he'd got a bargain and I expect he had. Everything had been renewed.

I think, all in all, that Gordon showed a lot of restraint in all our dealings with the Whaler. Some sort of outburst would have been understandable in any of the fixes we'd gotten into with her. But then Gordon's outbursts never come when you'd expect them.

DIARY

For these few minutes before our swim, Ginny has been intent on depositing her most unsettling thoughts with me. Since these unburdening sessions have been going on all week, I'm having more than enough of playing the confessor. It is clear to me that I am not cut out to be a priest - or I suppose I should say *priestess*.

Ginny says she has simply got to share these upsetting bits and pieces with someone sympathetic while she is on holiday, far away from people she knows. Telling me, a stranger, fragments of her personal life which trouble her is, she has admitted, a tremendous relief, freeing her from breaking down and confiding in a friend or neighbor, people who in the past have proven indiscreet.

Her husband, she tells me, won't listen to her. She excuses him partially by explaining that he really hasn't time because he's so busy treating his patients and counselling parishioners at the mission. Still, she complains that he expects her to be a model housekeeper, cook, wife and mother ALL THE TIME - uncomplaining, even and sunny, though not so spontaneously sunny that she calls attention to herself.

Having no one to confide in at home, she tells me, meant that her diary became the repository of her doubts, fears, anger and disillusionments, as well as her hopes and joys. Until recently, that is.

"Now though," she says, "I feel I mustn't record incidents which bother me, mustn't write down unpleasant, uncertain or critical observations - even really exuberant or upbeat ones. George, you see, doesn't approve of diaries where people express views they don't dare talk about. He preaches - he's a lay preacher, you know, when he's not practising chiropractic - that we must cultivate only evenness and good thoughts, scrapping the bad feelings and trimming the rough edges. 'Like a garden,' he says, 'where you pull out the weeds, keep the rows even, and cut back the tall grass around the perimeters.' Not, by the way, that George cares for gardening, especially weeding.

"Anyway, lately I've gone back and cut a lot of stuff - well, mostly everything - out of my diaries. Since I've done this I feel I have to be so careful about what I put down that I've pretty much lost interest in writing. That leaves me feeling sort of high and dry - almost like I don't have a life because I can't write about it. And the parts I've cut out seem like major amputations. Funny, I'd never have thought a diary could seem so important."

* * *

While I am racking my brains for a soothing and reasonable response, Ginny's mood changes. I should be getting used to this.

She jumps up smiling and briskly dusts the sand from her backside. "Swim time now," she announces cheerily, like the camp swimming instructor she has told me she once was.

"Have to get my mile in before George is ready to go

back to the bungalow.... Look! He's way out to the reef already. I'd better get going. He expects me to be finished my swim when he is."

Then, because I haven't responded, haven't budged, she adds, "Better hurry up and get in the water yourself. You don't want to miss the drive back. Five miles is too far to walk in this heat."

I get up slowly and trudge down towards the bay, hoping that the salt water will wash away my mounting anger and frustration. I tell myself that I shouldn't react to Ginny's moods, shouldn't forget either that she doesn't expect me to come up with solutions since she figures her problems are unsolvable. Nevertheless, I am amazed at how satisfied and briefly cleansed she seems after having transferred her worries to me - and how stressed I have become. I am genuinely sorry that she has dispensed with her diary, for my sake as much as hers.

Since our drive to this daily swim is the reason Gordon and I have associated with Ginny and George all week, I quicken my pace in anticipation of my immersion in the water I find so therapeutic. Gordon is already far out, cutting through the waves with his strong, regular and streamlined strokes. George has kicked his way out on his surfboard. He'll come in lying down on it, not standing up like the young Hawaiians - but then he's not young or Hawaiian, any more than we are.

As I enter the water I watch Ginny who is already travelling at her usual determined pace across the bay, not out towards the reef. She wears light, shortened flippers and small paddle-like mittens so that she continues to move much more quickly than she could without these appendages. It seems to me that, despite her paraphernalia and bravado, she is not a better swimmer than I am, and, although I am competent, I am not about to set any records.

It is Gordon who is the outstanding swimmer, though

neither George nor Ginny acknowledges his incredible prowess in this department. Anyway, we all love the water and it is this bond which has brought the four of us together and kept us associating - well, that and the fact that they have a car, that we couldn't afford to rent one, and that they have generously insisted we come along on their daily visit to this lovely, secluded spot. We're all agreed that the pool alongside the bungalows is much too tiny and crowded, and disappointed that the ocean in front is forbidden to swimmers at this time of year on account of the dangerous tidal surges which break over massive, though only intermittently-disclosed, rocks.

As I have anticipated, the salt water has its usual soothing effect on me, but I do not relax so completely as in the waters I am more used to. Here the waves are higher and stronger than at home in the Northumberland Straits, though the water temperature is about the same as it is there in August.

I cannot help worrying about the possibility that dangerous creatures may lurk beneath the surface here. Sharks perhaps - though I tell myself that the reef across the mouth of this bay should keep them out. Well, most of them. Perhaps not all. I recall that George has swum out over the reef with his board and come back in again, so why, I wonder, couldn't a George-sized shark do the same thing?

Still, I remind myself, the ocean in front of our Nova Scotia place was choked with ice cakes when we left and will still be caught in winter's icy grip long after our return, so I had better enjoy this last plunge. Tomorrow we start for home.

Like Ginny, I swim parallel to the shore - across the bay, not out. But because I am somewhat daunted by the height and power of the waves and the possibility, however remote, of encountering a shark, I stay closer to shore.

The only other people in sight are a young Hawaiian couple. The man, who is built like a sumo wrestler, is chest deep in the water spearing fish. You can see he has done this before. He is quick and adept, depositing his catch in a mesh bag he carries. The woman, a svelte, lithe beauty is swimming near him. Although it is obvious that she is completely at home in the water, she does not go far out. It seems to me that she is watchful, but perhaps that is just my imagination.

* * *

George is on his way in again on his board. He has caught a powerful wave which deposits him close to the Hawaiian girl. It is clear to me that she has caught his eye and he wants to have a closer look at her. He calls out to her. She turns away, pretending not to hear, but, since George bellows, it is impossible not to hear him.

George is apparently undeterred by the girl having cut him. He appears as determined to strike up an acquaintance with her as he was to meet Gordon and me the day of our arrival at the bungalows - though I suspect his intent is different in this instance. He has been attempting to convert Gordon all week, after giving up on me, but religious conversion is not, I suspect, the motivation driving George to accost this dark beauty.

Suddenly I am aware of a presence close at hand. I have been so absorbed watching George's performance that I have forgotten about Ginny, Gordon, and even the imagined shark.

After a second's panic, I see that it is Ginny who is bobbing close beside me, treading water. Her gaze, like mine, is directed toward George.

"That's exactly how *I* met George," she says with a catch in her voice. "Off a beach in California - not far from where we live now. I was just seventeen. He called me his favorite mermaid."

Ginny pauses and gulps, then turns to me.

"But he's come across a lot of favorite mermaids since then," she goes on, sounding increasingly breathless, so that I wonder whether, besides trying to comfort her in this unsuitable environment, I'm going to have to practise lifesaving techniques I learned so long ago that I am unsure whether I can make them work.

As we sink into a trough between waves and I look up to make sure I can ride up on the next crest, I see that Gordon is bearing down on us, going flat out as if his life depended on reaching shore. He interrupts his headlong rush to call out to us.

"Shark ... I think," he shouts and is off again.

In an instant Ginny regains control. Taking a deep breath, she races after Gordon, aqua flippers and mittens propelling her shoreward. I follow, but cannot keep up. If there really is a shark, I think, I'm the one it will take: these will be my last few seconds before death or dismemberment.

But instead of panicking, of seeing my entire life flash before my eyes as I've been told tends to occur under such threatening circumstances, I feel surprisingly calm - fatalistic, I suppose you'd call my state of mind. I even look to my right to see what George and the Hawaiian couple are up to. They cannot, I think, have heard Gordon's hoarse shout. I'm pretty sure it didn't carry much beyond Ginny and me.

I am right. The young man is still spearing fish while the girl swims nearby. George is kicking his way out toward the reef again.

* * *

Later, on this, our last evening, we have promised to play Syzygy with George and Ginny. We wanted to opt out, but they had already invited another couple, and Gordon and I thought we couldn't disappoint them by not turning up with the game, which belongs to us.

"So these folks think they saw a shark in the bay this afternoon," George bellows as he lets us into their bungalow. Ginny and the other couple smile vacuously and wait to see what we will say.

"Just a small one," Gordon says disparagingly, spreading out his arms sideways to indicate that the fish he saw was about four feet long. He has told me privately that he is unsure whether the fish which swam under him was actually a shark. "I didn't hang around to scrutinize it," he says.

It is clear that Gordon really doesn't want to discuss the incident, that he wishes someone would change the subject.

"Well, is everyone ready to play Syzygy?" I ask with faked enthusiasm.

"Sure thing!" George responds. "Just watch me win."

"George nearly always wins at Scrabble, which is quite a lot like Syzygy, I think," Ginny announces, smiling up at George.

But George does not win this first game and he is clearly put out. Gordon has won: he is a whiz at word games, which is not surprising since he is a writer and an English professor, though George and Ginny do not know this.

George and Ginny are too self-focused to have asked about our lives, though it is clear they assume that what we do is unimportant since we have not volunteered any information about our doings. Besides, when, on our first meeting, they inquired where we came from and we said *Atlantic Canada ... the Maritimes ...* their startled reaction indicated that, if they had had such a skeleton in their closet they would never have let it out. Our neck of the woods is clearly, by their reckoning, third world, or nearly. This assumption is, I suppose, substantiated by the fact that on this trip we cannot afford to rent a car. We have not explained that this is because we have just built a forty-foot-long screened porch onto our house which overlooks one of the world's loveliest unspoiled and unfrequented beaches.

*   *   *

Gordon and I are ready to go back to our bungalow. We need to pack our few belongings tonight since the taxi which is taking us to the island airport is coming for us at daybreak.

But George insists on having one more game of Syzygy. He has turned over all the letters and wild counters and begun choosing his. While he is moving some of the wooden squares around with a pretence of circulating them, I notice that his left hand holds down a considerable number which do not move. I look around the table to see if anyone else has observed this. Gordon is talking with the other couple. None of them is looking at the table.

But Ginny has seen what has happened. She looks across at me, and then away. She is embarrassed that I have witnessed George's cheating, though in her confessions she has told me that George often cheats. She has also remarked that no one else seems to notice.

George wins this final game. Small wonder! He has glommed onto most of the wild squares.

Before we leave George and Ginny's bungalow, I would like to take Ginny aside and advise her to go back to writing in her diary, that it will be a comfort to get her troubles off her chest in this way. But then I think: *what if George did find her scribblings? What would he do?* And I decide that she is probably right to fear the consequences. So I do not do or say anything.

*   *   *

On our long flights home I confide this tale of Ginny and George to *my* diary because I find that what I have seen of them troubles me. But, as I write, I pause to think of what Ginny has said about making upsetting disclosures in a diary, her concern about who might read her commentaries - and I wonder.

CASINO

Ever since the opening of a casino quite near here, Arnold has bellyached about the perils - "evils," to quote him - of gambling. He's gone on and on and on about gambling being "a terrible modern social disease" and "another curse of civilization right on our doorstep." When on that tack he's begun to sound like one of those strident old-time evangelists.

It's casinos more than horse races, dog races or lotteries which particularly rile him. They've grabbed and held his attention for months now. If I hadn't known better, I'd have sworn he'd been making a study of the subject - keeping tabs particularly on new casinos opening in what he considers to be out-of-the-way parts of the world like ours. I used to think he kept informed through the internet.

Earlier this week, over supper, he introduced me to his latest find. "You know what, Aline?" he announced, pausing briefly to make sure he had my undivided attention before filling me in. "They've opened two new casinos way up there in Nova Scotia. A shame. While the politicians pushed to have them, lots of the locals protested, saying that casinos would spoil the quality of life.

"Bring in whores and criminals too, the Mounties predicted. The organizers brag they've booked cruise ships full of would-be gamblers into Halifax for the entire season.... And, when the tourists get worn out operating one-armed bandits and playing blackjack, they get packed onto buses and carted off to view authentic *Titanic* graves. Now isn't that whole thing sick?"

Although Arnold took a few seconds' breather, I knew he didn't expect an answer. He is a talker by nature, a *serious* talker, so when I say he goes on about something, I really mean it. On and on ... and on. Just try to stop him. Not that I ever consider attempting to shut him up any more. When he's on a roll, so to speak, he blows up if I interject even a few words.

"Don't interrupt me," he blusters. "I'll lose my train of thought."

"One could only hope," I used to imagine saying, laughingly. But I never plucked up the courage to venture making this or any other such quip out loud at these seemingly critical times. Arnold's temper is too uncertain. He wouldn't be amused.

Years ago when the children were little I resigned myself to the fact that Arnold is a monologist rather than a conversationalist. He can be very entertaining in this capacity when he's not pontificating at length about his current pet peeve - like this gambling business.

Actually, I couldn't understand why he latched onto this particular hobbyhorse. He's smart and mostly balanced. In fact, in some departments, I find him quite perspicacious.

Because of this, I'd expect him to see the irony in a farmer like himself singling out this specific human frailty to vent his spleen on. If you searched the world over, it would be hard - well, impossible, is more like it - to find a more uncertain occupation than ours, one that's a bigger gamble. Where else, I wonder, could you turn up more unpredictable odds?

That's saying a lot because the older I get the more often I'm forced to realize that just about everything in life is a gamble. Birth, death, marriage. All dicey ventures, the last perhaps the most chancy because at first it seems controllable.

* * *

For months now, I've been dying to tease Arnold about being a gambler at heart. I'd love to point out that he seems to enjoy speculating - or at least watching me speculate - in our farming enterprises. Not all of them, certainly, but some that no one else around here would touch with the proverbial ten foot pole.

It's true he plants the traditional corn and beans like our neighbors, but instead of hogs or cattle we've got sheep. Expensive, imported hair sheep at that - sheep only a handful of people in the entire country have, and they're either working at universities with subsidized experimental agricultural facilities or rich enough to be able to afford a risky flutter.

"Yes, they're our woolless wonders," Arnold has quipped, apparently unruffled, when responding to our neighbors' jibes. Though I suspect that underneath his bravado he's been, by times, somewhat embarrassed about having all those sheep running around the creekside pasture and the even bigger field which by rights everyone else *knows* should be in corn or beans, he's never let on even to me that he's ever had any doubts.

"They're Aline's sheep," he's told everyone who's persisted in making snide remarks and asking impertinent questions. "If you want to know anything about them, ask her. She's got all the answers."

And, oddly enough, it's clear he believes I have. For all the explosive temper and touchiness he can demonstrate from time to time over pretty insignificant matters, he's never once lost his cool or tackled me about these sheep. That I find really hard to comprehend because, although I've always believed in this venture, from the beginning I've recognized it for the gamble it is - or was up till recently when it's begun to pay off handsomely. For months I could hardly sleep for worrying - and sleeping was always one of my long suits, a seemingly indestructible talent I figured I'd been born with.

Several times in desperation - and despite Arnold's protests - I even had several lengthy long-distance heart-to-heart telephone conversations with Ruth, my former college roommate and still my best friend, about my worries over this investment. "It's a long shot," I told her. "Thinking I can sell sheep - expensive hair sheep, no wool, from a base in a part of the country where cattle and hogs are top meat animals - is crazy. Isn't it?" I'd ask, half serious, half laughing.

Like Arnold, Ruth believes steadfastly in my abilities. She insisted I wouldn't lose. "You've always had wonderful ideas, Aline. And they always work out. Quit worrying. Sell the damn sheep over the internet."

Ruth's reiterated faith in my judgment comforted me somewhat, though really our conversations were generally spoiled by the ruckus Arnold raised under the kitchen window near where the phone is. One after the other, he revved up chain saw, shop vac and lawn mower. Then, when I hung up, he came in and lectured me about the expense and frivolity of personal long-distance calls.

When he did this I was all set to sound off about what I think is such unfair nagging. Instead, I reminded myself how Arnold has never once complained about the more than $20,000 he borrowed to buy what he's described simply as "those fancy genetics" - the embryos and semen imported and introduced into our recipient ewes by a high-priced team of experts. I am grateful and so touched by his trusting my judgment in this department that I can't find it in me to turn on him. Nevertheless, I'm absolutely stymied when I try to fathom how a person who gets so uptight and disagreeable about trivial aggravations seems so laid back and supportive about such a major investment and nerve-racking gamble as these imported sheep. Increasingly, as I go about my household, barn and pasture chores, pondering this to me inexplicable paradox, I've decided that sheep are much easier to comprehend than human beings. No contest.

I also wondered secretly if Arnold hadn't enjoyed this gamble. Although he'd never used that word, his choice of expressions nonetheless gave me pause. Months ago, when he thought I was 'down' and wanted to console me, he said, "Don't you worry, Honey, there's gonna be a big pay-out one of these days. We'll hit the jackpot. I'd bet everything I've got any day on your brains and know-how."

Now, if you'd overheard a stranger make these comments, wouldn't you imagine he was a gambler? Perhaps even a frequenter of casinos?

*   *   *

After all Arnold's talk about casinos being such dens of iniquity I must admit I began to acquire a rather perverse yen to visit one - preferably the new one near here whose opening had so incensed him. Not that I was much interested in playing the various games. I was just curious. I wanted to see what was what.

I never expected to get the chance. My going there happened without my ever lifting a finger one summer evening while Arnold was off delivering sheep.

Ever since the sheep have begun to sell for between one and five thousand dollars each, Arnold has become a willing part-time trucker. He's hauled trailer loads most often south to the Texas border-crossing to Mexico at Brownsville. He has also gone north, beyond the Canadian border into Saskatchewan and Manitoba. He's even driven east several times to Massachusetts, Virginia and Florida - though never west over the mountains. Californians have come to us.

Ruth was right about the internet. That's where most of this business has come from.

Ruth and I now tended to exchange calls while Arnold was off on these trips. I was lonelier when he'd gone than I would have expected. I thought I'd find his brief absences a relief. I did for about a day and then the house began to seem oppressively quiet. Ruth knew this, so on Arnold's last trip South, she phoned to tell me that she and Jack were going through here on their way to California and would like to stop by to see me.

"We'll get there by seven. But don't make dinner, Aline," she insisted. "Jack and I have a surprise for you. We're taking you out to a new place. It's not your run-of-the-mill restaurant. But we hear the food's great. There's entertainment too. Tell you more when we see you."

* * *

When Ruth and Jack picked me up they still didn't disclose our destination, didn't want to talk about it.

"Why so tight-lipped?" I asked.

Jack just laughed. "You'll see presently: it's only about a half hour's drive," was all he said. He looked pretty pleased with himself.

Ruth was wearing that exasperating Mona Lisa smile which I know from past experience means that you might as well try to pry a secret out of that famous painting as pester her for an answer.

And so, as we drove into the dusk, we talked of other

things - mostly the children, theirs and ours.

The first CASINO signs were discreet, but, as we approached the entrance, huge letters and arrows, lit and flashing, made certain that no passerby could miss the place. As Jack turned off and followed the arrows at a snail's pace to a parking place not that easy to find amidst the sea of cars, trucks (some still attached to animal trailers), vans, RV's, buses and semis - I struggled to conceal my disbelief and uneasiness.

What was Arnold going to say when he found out about this junket? He'd find it hard to believe I hadn't planned it with Ruth - scheduling it for when he was off on the road. I felt sure he wouldn't listen to my explanation. Even if he did, I had to admit that the truth in this instance was hard to believe.

As I climbed out of the back seat of the *Pathfinder*, guilt, anger and excitement vied for supremacy. While I was pleased to be here and curious about what I'd see, I nevertheless felt guilty as a well-meaning teenager who, in going out for an evening with her friends, has unintentionally gone against her parents' wishes by turning up at a place they'd disapprove of. At the same time I was angry that, at my age and with a considerable amount of education and sophistication, I felt like this. Furious with myself too for caring so much about Arnold's opinions - including his silly prejudices - and furious with Arnold for having plied me with such cut-and-dried views about things I was sure he knew nothing about.

These angry fragmented thoughts coursed through my mind in jig time. I knew I had to banish them promptly for the time being. Put on a good face. Not spoil everyone's time. Not only Orientals, I thought as I turned to Ruth and Jack, forcing a smile in the white light of the overhead lamp, are concerned with saving face.

I guess I wasn't altogether successful. Ruth guessed that something was amiss with me.

"You okay?" she asked, touching my sweatered arm lightly.

"Yes, fine," I answered. "Just excited and curious. Hungry too."

True, but not the whole truth.

* * *

The restaurant was at the far end of the establishment - between the sprawling casino and the adjoining hotel. Apart from the security guards at the entrance, no one appeared to notice us. On the long walk down one of the wide aisles, not a single person looked up from the slot machines or card tables. Only the servers of water, coffee and complimentary cold drinks nodded as we passed.

No booze appeared on their trolleys, though. So Arnold had been wrong about most casino customers being sloshed. No alcohol was being served or consumed here.

That didn't mean that the customers weren't high. Most seemed to be in a trancelike state. Zombie-like they fed their money or tokens into voracious one-armed bandits, seemingly transfixed by the possibility that their machines were about to cough up quantities of change into the gutters below - "silver" they (and we) could in fact hear cascading here and there to left and right, noisy as hailstones in the eaves-troughing during a sudden, violent storm.

Off to the far left where the long, high card tables stood apart, silence reigned. In my glancing assessment of what was happening at these, I saw no traces of the conviviality I had expected. It didn't look to me as if anyone was having much fun. Certainly there appeared to be little light-hearted camaraderie.

The restaurant, like the pool alongside, at the hotel's

entrance from the casino, was kidney-shaped and inviting to look at. But, whereas the pool was small and empty, the restaurant was huge and full. A long line of hopeful would-be eaters had formed outside. It snaked down an avenue which led to side rooms filled with more machines. We joined the line.

In contrast to the rather somber atmosphere in the casino, the mood in the lineup was upbeat. Most of the expectant patrons seemed to have eaten here before and been convinced that the food was well worth waiting for. Enthusiastically they discussed the merits of the various posted all-you-could-eat entrees and peeped down through the glass separating them from the diners to check the color and texture of beef cut from the hip-of-beef visible in the distance and the seafood laid out in appealing proximity.

They knew that there was no danger of this food emporium running out of either basics or delicacies or closing early like the local restaurants in the surrounding farm-based towns. This elaborate cafeteria, like the casino, was in business twenty-four hours a day - except Sundays.

*   *   *

Although the food was as good as everyone said, I was tired when we finished eating. It was after nine and bedtime for anyone who'd been up and doing chores since 5 a.m. as I had. I think Ruth was tired too - though she wouldn't say so - but Jack seemed to be revved up, eager to try his luck at the machines and tables. I think really he wanted to get away from Ruth and me for a bit, guessing that we were tired, not serious about gambling, and about to say we were ready to leave for home.

So while Jack made a beeline for the card tables, Ruth and I headed to the cashiers' counter to buy $20 worth of quarters, nickels and tokens - the limit we'd set ourselves for playing the machines.

To my surprise, for about half an hour I quite enjoyed myself. Ruth and I, sitting side by side on the stools before our machines, fed in our money and were, from time to time, rewarded by a tumbling flood of quarters, just enough to encourage us to persist, not enough to break even. We laughed about our new-found status as gamblers - and losers - until our scowling neighbors reminded us that for them this was no light-hearted flutter, no laughing matter either.

"Let's go find Jack," I suggested. "I've had enough. How about you?"

Ruth nodded through the smoky haze which blanketed the room, and we set off in search of Jack. Finding him was not going to be easy. Foolishly, we'd forgotten to arrange a time or place of meeting.

As we scanned the faces at the machines and tables, we heard the loudspeaker proclaiming the departures of buses for various nearby towns and cities and saw passengers detach themselves reluctantly from their machines and move towards the exits.

Suddenly, as I was idly scanning the crowds, my heart constricted so I felt I could scarcely breathe. I stood absolutely still, trembling. Ruth, who was walking ahead continued talking, assuming doubtless that I was still with her. When she realized I wasn't there, she turned around, then hurried back to me.

"Hey there, Kiddo, what's happened? You look like you've seen a ghost. All that rosy outdoors color of yours is gone. Come and sit down."

But all the nearby seats were taken.

"Oh, I'm okay," I whispered. "Just the smoke and crowds, I think. I've got to get outside into the air. If only we could find Jack."

And suddenly there he was beside us, grinning and exuberant. "I won," he crowed. "Must have over $100. Got to change the loot into cash to carry.... How 'bout you girls?"

"Losers both," we chorused.

And that was that. Ruth and I made our way back to the *Pathfinder*. Jack joined us a few minutes later and we were soon on our way back to the farm. Ruth didn't ask me again about the "spell" I'd had. And I decided not to explain. I had to think about what I'd seen, figure out how I was going to deal with it.

* * *

Arnold had been at one of those card tables. Arnold – my husband who'd lectured me about how much he hated gambling, especially at casinos - was playing cards in the very casino he'd so maligned. He had not looked up when I'd stopped to stare. He'd seemed absolutely focused on his hand. If I hadn't seen him with my own eyes I'd never have taken anyone else's word that he'd been there.

In the humming darkness of the *Pathfinder*'s back seat, I tried to make sense out of what I'd seen. I couldn't.

I was thankful, though, for the darkness and the sound of motor and tires, which exempted me from making polite conversation till we got back to the farm. At least Arnold wouldn't be there - yet. But when he did return what was I going to say?

Nothing. Nothing yet.

THE BED

This bed is the last remaining piece of furniture in my mother's house. A mahogany four-poster, it is monumentally solid and heavy - a major impediment to moving. But then, it dates from an era when most people stayed put, when such a substantial possession set the tone for a permanent and predictable lifestyle. My mother has had this bed in the same place in the same room since her marriage seventy-two years ago. Before that, it was in her grandmother's house for goodness knows how long.

"Be sure you hang onto that bed when I'm gone," she has insisted over the years. "It's valuable, a family heirloom. I want David to have it for his house when he marries."

For several reasons I never paid much attention to these frequent and pressing reminders. First and foremost, I haven't been able to imagine my mother *gone*: her personality has been dominant for so long, even when she's not actually present. In our house almost a thousand miles from here I still imagine her responding to nearly everything I say or do - usually critically.

Then there's David - *Adonis*, as my mother has by times fondly referred to her only grandson ever since he turned seventeen - who has shown no serious interest in matrimony or acquisitions which might anchor him. "I'm going to wait to get married till I'm sure about everything," he has remarked off-handedly when pressed. "And right now I don't want to be tied down by a lot of stuff."

So I'm not holding my breath until he decides to settle down. From my present vantage point I can't imagine David, or anyone else for that matter, having *everything* resolved any time soon. I'm almost sixty and I'm still not close to reaching that state of enviable certainty about *anything*.

Now, though, the unimaginable has happened. My mother is *gone* - well almost. What I mean is she's not in this house any more and her once extraordinarily strong spirit and mind have almost vacated her now frail and dwindling body. The time has come for me to make decisions about her affairs. What to do with this bed? is the question facing me right now.

The Dutch antique store owner who has bought most of the furniture keeps badgering me about the bed - and gradually upping the ante. He is well aware that it is by far the best piece in the house but would prefer I not know he knows. He has planted himself here in the hall and is bullying me to part with it.

I don't stand up well to being bullied, so I find myself vacillating - despite my mother's imagined voice exhorting me not to be weak-minded, not to give in. The main reason for my indecision, though, is that Gordon complained earlier this af-ternoon that dismantling this monster, loading it onto our old half-ton on top of the rest of the odds and ends I've saved, and trucking the entire unwieldy cargo all the way back to New Brunswick, will be the end of him. "My back's killing me al-ready," he complained.

Since Gordon has been surprisingly patient throughout this upheaval, I really don't want to put him through anything more. I certainly understand how he feels: I'm exhausted and fed up myself. And since I've always believed that people are much more important than possessions, I am on the point of abandoning the bed to this rude and pushy dealer when Gordon opens the screen door and confronts the wretched man.

"Mr. Van Dine," Gordon announces in his most authoritative voice, "we're keeping the bed. I'm ready to load it up now, so I guess you won't be wanting to stay here any longer."

Ordinarily, when Gordon assumes this blunt and commanding tone and stance, I cringe. If he confronts strangers in this way, I am embarrassed: if he treats me to such an unequivocal display of his power, I feel unsettled for days. Today, though, I find myself relaxing, even thanking the powers that be for sending Gordon in here in the nick of time, relieving me of the burden of making a decision and coping with this overbearing dealer. I know that Gordon will have the obnoxious man out of the house in short order. In a confrontation no man is a match for Gordon.

Nevertheless, Mr. Van Dine doesn't move at once. I think he is embarrassed to be compelled to back down so quickly, especially in front of me. I suppose he is racking his brains for a way to save face.

So Mr. Van Dine stands still. He and Gordon eye one another like two strange dogs contemplating a fight - or perhaps two roosters, I think as I watch this performance. Gordon squares his still-broad shoulders and draws himself up to his full height, so that he is now perhaps an inch taller than the dealer. Under Gordon's unbending and hostile gaze Mr. Van Dine seems to be shrinking slowly into his well-padded middle.

"Best be going now," he murmurs, pathetically trying to sound as if the decision is his. He sidles towards the door, eyes lowered, no longer the swaggering and assertive loudmouth of a few minutes ago.

When we hear Mr. Van Dine's van start up, Gordon is

still standing tall. He doesn't look like a man with a bad back. He is clearly proud of having won a battle and pleased me.

"Well, Elizabeth," he says in a gentler, though still assertive tone, "that's that settled. Now we'll be able to get along home. Just give me time to take this bed apart and load it. We'll be under way before you know it. Nobody's going to stand in our way now."

* * *

Perhaps one is ill-advised to make such categorical statements, because Gordon has no sooner disappeared into the bedroom than the screen door opens again; this time disclosing a frail and trembling old woman - my mother.

I don't move, don't believe my eyes. *Not possible that she's here*, I tell myself in these first incredibly unsettling instants. *We've already said good-bye to her. She could never get away from the home, never walk the half mile that separates the home from this house....*

I am almost convinced I've been granted a strange and improbable vision: maybe the second sight both my Celtic grandmothers believed in. It might not be so unreasonable, I reckon dizzily, for so strong a spirit as my mother's to have dispensed with convention and returned to haunt this house.

But she is real enough - present in the flesh, though tottering and about to fall as I pull myself together and rush forward to catch her.

I think she does not quite recognize me. I'd say she is vaguely aware that she has seen me before, but is uncertain about where or when. It is the house, not me, that holds what attention she can muster. It is clear that the familiar atmosphere of her front hall is comforting her, even beginning to restore some of her very meager strength.

Now that she has caught her breath, she struggles to escape my embrace. When she is free, she staggers down the long hall.

"Have to lie down," she whispers, hoarsely determined, struggling to say what she means. "In my own bed. It is my rest time."

Gordon's head pokes out from the bedroom. "What's all this?" he asks unnecessarily.

He is face to face with what is happening, but, like me, it is clear he is having difficulty crediting his faculties. Unlike me, though, he appears to have no temporary illusions about visions or hauntings.

He pulls himself together quickly and says in a guarded but firm voice, "So, Mother Cameron, what are you doing here? You're supposed to be at Cedar Crest."

My mother stops before Gordon and looks up at him hesitantly, like a child who has been caught misbehaving and is being reprimanded by her father for a misdemeanor she doesn't quite understand. She trembles. Then, glimpsing the bed, she tries to step around Gordon to get to it. She stumbles and almost falls.

Catching her, Gordon swoops her up and deposits her on the bed. Although he has made the only possible move, I can see his frustration and anger mounting. Already in a lather, beads of perspiration stand out on his forehead and his neck and ears are red.

He closes the bedroom door quietly and stalks down the hall past me without speaking. The screen door bangs as he steps out onto the porch. He won't find much relief there: it's hotter than inside.

For this out-of-control situation he obviously has no comfortable solution. Neither do I. I don't think there is one. But I am more used than he to uncertain positions.

Neither Gordon nor my mother can tolerate not being in control. I have always thought that with their incredible stamina, determination to have their own way and quick tempers they are a lot alike. That's why theirs has been a love/hate relationship from the beginning. My mother is the only person I know of who, in a contest of wills, has sometimes beaten Gordon. He has alternately admired and been exasperated by her because of this, though mostly he has tried to ignore her victories. Sometimes I think both of them have enjoyed these contests while they are taking place. Both of them, though, are sore losers.

Ordinarily, my inclination is to keep out of the way and avoid taking sides. This situation, however, is very different from those gone by. My mother cannot help herself: hers is a last ditch stand, instinctive and unreasoned as a sick animal's.

Confronted by this realization, Gordon clearly feels helpless, unable to cope with this defenseless and uncomprehending, but still stubborn, old woman. He's so hot and bothered because he feels mad and sad at the same time. Tired too, though he'd never admit it.

It's time I tried to do something. This kind of frustration is bad for Gordon's high blood pressure, and, although to me he mostly seems as strong and fit as ever, I know this is not exactly so.

I persuade him to sit down in a deck chair while I go inside to make him coffee - which is probably not what he should have, but what he'd like. I tell him that if we sit out here for half an hour while my mother sleeps, I'll drive her back to the home. I point out that these days she never sleeps more than half an hour at a time.

* * *

When my mother wakes up she seems disoriented. Apart

from the bed, the room is empty; the bureau, dressing table, even the curtains, gone. And because she is on it, she seems unaware of the familiar bed.

I help her up and as we walk slowly down the hall, past the empty rooms, she seems puzzled, a sleepwalker in unfamiliar territory.

Gordon comes with us to the truck. Because the cab is high off the ground, Gordon is about to lift my mother in. But she shakes her head and refuses his help.

"James," she says, "where did you get this old wreck? I can't go anywhere in it. What are you thinking of?"

Briefly, apart from confusing Gordon with my father, she sounds almost herself. But she cannot keep up her protest. She is about to collapse again.

Gordon lifts her up once more, depositing her in the passenger seat and then giving her a hug. Since Gordon rarely hugs anyone, I am surprised. He is calm and gentle now, but still firm.

My mother has relaxed. She tries to smile at Gordon.

"Elizabeth, you stay here," Gordon says to me. "I'm going to take her back. You're not up to this. She needs me."

So they go off down the road together, the contents of the box jouncing as the truck hits deep potholes across from the MacAlpine place. I go back to the deck chair to await Gordon's return.

I wish my mother could *go gentle into that good night*, but realize that this is not to be. Her heredity is against this happening. I think of what she once told me about her grandfather and his two brothers, newly arrived from Scotland, walking all the way from Digby, Nova Scotia to Ontario with their oxen, intent on finding the ideal land for homesteading. Finding it, they persevered. Giving up is not in her makeup, any more than it was in theirs.

TRUTH TO TELL

Truth to tell, we have had a most trying month. Now that July is nearly over, I'm not sure we can pick up again where we left off in the spring.

July and August are usually the best part of the year for us, as for most Maritimers, and we try to make the most of this special time. Since Gordon retired three years ago, we have divided our summers between our house near town and our seaside cottage, a two-hour drive distant, and, although it has sometimes been a struggle to keep everything going, Gordon and I have both felt it's worth carrying on like this as long as we can.

We have been buoyed up too by the fact that the children and grandchildren have clearly endorsed this state of affairs: they are, I'd say, comforted to know that there is always room for them at both these home bases and that our lives seem to be unfolding much as they always have.

Every other summer I teach a three week summer school, a literature half course, at the college where I formerly taught full-time - and this past summer was the year my summer school stint was scheduled. Although I have to travel thirty-five miles each way, the trip is worth the effort.

The drive through the awakened countryside gives me time to collect my thoughts, while savoring the subtle sun-simmered fragrances - wild strawberries, spruce sap, wild roses, clover - which drift in through the open windows, and viewing the changing banks of wayside flowers which from a distance look both stronger and more colorful than the tame varieties I have planted in my garden.

I also enjoy meeting a new crop of students and renewing acquaintance with former colleagues who have not yet retired. Besides, with the extra money from this brief return to academe, I have the wherewithal to splurge a little; to buy several elegant sheets and pillowcases or a pair or two of curtains to spruce up either the home place or the cottage, and perhaps a learning 'toy' such as a beginner's microscope or telescope for our ten-year-old grandson. Sometimes I also treat myself to a special dress or skirt which I might otherwise consider extravagant.

This past summer, though, we had to scrap most of our usual pursuits - summer school excepted - because former acquaintances, and would-be acquaintances, from distant places and times long past descended on us in quick succession. A final encounter before we all drop dead - with the added bonus, for them, of a free vacation - appeared to be what they had in mind.

All these people seemed intent on assessing close up the state of our health, our finances, our progeny and our accomplishments - in comparison with their own. Since they had retired and either downsized their own establishments or moved into single bedroom apartments, they had time and money, they told us, to travel the world. Our problem with this arrangement was that four couples all made a beeline for our place, where, on arrival, they remarked gleefully how nice it was that we still had plenty of room for guests. Fortunately - or maybe unfortunately, because a crowd might have discouraged some of these intruders - they didn't all arrive at the same time.

Despite our best efforts to dissuade them, none of these unwelcome visitors would take no for an answer. When we tried to deter them by saying we were busy - with summer school, family arriving on and off all summer and extended absences at our not-easily-accessible island cottage - they turned a deaf ear. Arriving just before dinner, they were intent on staying.

It wasn't even as if these insistent guests - with the exception of one half of one couple - were now, or had ever been, friends. This single exception was Gordon's boyhood friend, but neither of us had seen him for years or met his new wife. Two of the other couples were casual acquaintances, and the remaining duo, a second cousin and his English wife, people we didn't know existed and had never met until they knocked on our front door.

* * *

The first couple, Josh and Janet McDougall, arrived unannounced on Canada Day. When they pulled into our driveway, they were hauling a tent trailer and told us they were just dropping by to say hello, that they reckoned there weren't many of their old friends still left in town. They were, they added, in this first enthusiastic greeting, spending the summer camping. What we didn't realize then was that for the past month they had been camping all across the country in their acquaintances' yards, as close to the back or front doors as possible. Naively, we also didn't pick up on the fact that our place was their immediate campground choice.

Since my summer school was due to start the day after the McDougalls' unheralded arrival, I thought we'd give them dinner and then send them on their way early. *Don't worry about eating and running*, I imagined myself saying. *We're busy people and I need to get a good night's sleep because I begin teaching summer school tomorrow.*

Since we had only a passing acquaintance with Josh and Janet, I didn't think getting rid of them would be a problem. Although they had lived in our town years ago, we had never spent any time with them then. We didn't really have anything in common and in the past had found we quickly exhausted small talk in lineups at the bank, post office or grocery store.

But after several pre-dinner drinks, conversation didn't seem to be a problem. Well, I guess *conversation* is the wrong word because it suggests give and take. The McDougalls' forte, when imbibing, turned out to be monologues - long, tedious ones. When, early on, we ran out of liquor, and I said it was time to eat, Josh insisted on going out to their car for more booze.

"Just one more drink before we eat," he pleaded. "It's been a long, hot day.... A long time no see you folks either," he added after a pause, gulping, his speech already slurred.

I began to worry. How could either Josh or Janet drive after so large an infusion of intoxicants? How would they get to the local trailer park and set up their tent trailer in their increasingly addled state?

They couldn't of course, and by the time Gordon and I were beginning to realize we were stuck for the night with this increasingly unwelcome couple, Janet announced unapologetically that they'd have to camp here - *just for tonight, of course.* "Anyway, that won't be a problem. You've got lots of room."

"Sure thing!" Josh agreed. " Must be four ... five acres. Not to mention all those bedrooms upstairs." Then he added, "Hey, Gordy," (and nobody who really knows Gordon calls him *Gordy*) "how 'bout giving me a hand setting up our camper."

An ultimatum, not a question.

I excused myself and went upstairs to bed. I had trouble sleeping, though. There was a lot of door slamming and stomping around the house, upstairs and down. Then our pump ran nonstop while the McDougalls showered, calling out raucously to one another over the sound of the endlessly cascading water.

When they finally settled into their camper, they turned on a blindingly bright light which illuminated the entire back of the house, including the bedroom where I was trying to sleep. When I looked out the window to assess the situation, I could see that their power source was the electric outlet over our back door. They had removed our shade and bulb to attach their umbilical cord.

* * *

The next morning ... and the next ... and the next, I slunk out of the house very early, without breakfast, using the front door to avoid disturbing the McDougalls, afraid they would intercept me - remind me again not to forget to pick up the odds and ends they'd requested the preceding evening. They'd said they needed extra supplies to entertain the friends from town they had invited to the noontime barbecues they held in our back yard or on the sheltered lawn down by the lake. They never did invite us to any of their dos.

Every day when I returned from the college, I couldn't believe that Gordon hadn't gotten rid of the McDougalls. He's never been one to suffer fools gladly, or even put up with shenanigans from the children or grandchildren, but the McDougalls had him stymied.

I'd heard a few of his ineffectual attempts to send them on their way, but these polite, though pointed, suggestions didn't appear to sink in. I figured this was at least partly because, soon after getting up just before noon, Josh and Janet began drinking.

While the McDougalls were using our place as if it belonged to them and I was off at the college, Gordon retreated to the barn he was building. Clearly, he found that, in flooring what was to be the loft, he was able to recapture a measure of sanity. He told me one evening when he took me out to admire his day's work that, if the McDougalls came to the bottom of the ladder, he told them not to come up, that it wasn't safe. Apparently, Gordon also pretended he couldn't hear anything if they called up. This was undoubtedly the truth, because whenever Josh or Janet hove in sight, he started up the power saw.

From this floor-in-the-making, Gordon had a bird's eye view of the property - a sort of treetop deck. So far, he hadn't gotten around to putting up the second story walls and roof, not even the uprights, so the view in all directions was marvelous, and unobstructed.

Although Gordon made do after a fashion during the day, in the evenings when he came inside, he acted increasingly morose. Most people would easily have translated his tense and scowling silence as hostility. Not the McDougalls. Breezing in just in time for dinner, they chattered away, apparently oblivious of our disenchantment with the status quo.

Josh wasn't even really put out when Gordon flatly refused to teach him how to cope with the hardly-more-than-a-bathtub-sized fiberglass sailboat he'd brought with him, strapped on the car roof. Although Gordon loves sailing and would, under more auspicious circumstances, have jumped at the opportunity to drop his hammer and go out on the water, this time he excused himself on the grounds that he couldn't take time off from the barn building. "Got to finish it before winter," he insisted. "Abby's counting on it."

"No problem," Josh said. "I'm not worried. Can't be

much to sailing a little tub like mine on a tiny lake like this. A piece of cake, I'd say. Not like the big boats both our kids have on the salt water out West. I'm gonna get a forty footer too when I get home.... Surprised you haven't got one.

"Anyhow, just thought I'd practise up on this little dinghy where it's real safe."

Gordon tried to warn Josh about the unsteadiness and unpredictability of the wind on our lake. As a neighbor of ours observed one late June afternoon, "That wind blowin' from the southwest sure is comin' from all directions."

After the neighbor had gone, Gordon and I laughed at what seemed a nonsensical observation. But the truth is, as we've admitted since, the neighbor was not exactly wrong: the surrounding hills catch the wind and bounce it back over the water so it is impossible to predict where it's coming from. These oddly swirling breezes, interspersed with moments of calm, mean that, although the lake is small and appears safe, boating here can be tricky. Anyone sailing or windsurfing needs to be cautious and experienced. So despite the fact that the lake is ringed with houses, hardly anyone, apart from ourselves, sails or windsurfs on it.

* * *

The accident occurred mid-afternoon during the last week of summer school.

For the first time since the McDougalls' arrival Gordon and I felt relaxed. Standing up on the newly-laid loft floor alongside our daughter Abby, we were warmed by the sun and cooled by an increasingly strong breeze. We gazed out across the garden and trees to the lake where whitecaps were ruffling the surface. Not a soul was visible. Josh and Janet were down by the water, screened by the spruces and maples - out of sight and almost out of mind.

Abby had the afternoon off from the vet clinic where she practises, and had come home for a swim and a visit. She was keen to inspect the barn too: her horse Elsa is to be its first occupant.

Abby hadn't been home since the McDougalls' arrival, so when she saw a pudgy woman emerging, screaming, from the arc of trees which protects our swimming place, and laboring up the hillside towards the barn, she looked dumbfounded.

"Help! ... Help!" Janet screeched. "Josh's tipped over," she yelled up.... "He's gonna drown... Do somethin'... Hurry... He can't swim."

From our treetop platform we looked back over the lake, and, sure enough, almost halfway across was Josh's capsized yellow dinghy with someone - presumably Josh - clinging to it. Momentarily, we were dazed, caught completely off guard by what had happened.

Abby was the first to recover. Before Gordon or I could move, she was down the ladder and racing towards the water. Gordon and I followed at a slower pace. There was a time when Gordon would have made it down the hill at least as quickly as Abby - but not since he broke his ankle about twelve years ago.

By the time we got to the beach Abby had almost reached Josh and the dinghy. Like Gordon, she is a tremendously strong swimmer.

At Abby's approach, Josh lunged out and grabbed her. Gordon and I watched in horror while Abby wrestled with the panicked man. With both our boats on the island, we had no rescue craft.

Not waiting to witness the outcome of Abby's struggle with Josh, Gordon ditched his sandals, dived off the wharf and struck out for the yellow boat. When he got there, both Abby and Josh were underwater. They surfaced just as Gordon reached them.

Letting go of Abby, Josh made a grab for Gordon. But with both Abby and himself at risk - not to mention Josh - Gordon evidently decided he wasn't going to fool around making moves which might prove ineffectual. Rising up out of the water like Proteus, he struck Josh, apparently knocking him unconscious. Then before Josh could sink again or come to, Gordon flipped him onto his back and began towing him to shore. Abby, treading water near the capsized boat, soon began pushing it toward shore.

Janet, standing beside me at the end of the wharf, and somewhat recovered now that the situation seemed under control, began to swear and threaten. "Goddam son of a bitch. You saw him. That bastard hit Josh. We're gonna sue. Our son's a lawyer. You just wait."

By the time Gordon hauled him up on the beach, Josh had come to.

"Could do with a drink after all that," he announced shakily as he took in the situation. "How 'bout..."

Gordon didn't let him finish. "No. Enough's enough. Time to get ready and hit the road. Janet can drive if you don't feel up to it today. We'll help pack up your gear."

And that was that. It was apparent to everyone that Gordon was not going to back down this time.

When the McDougalls pulled out of our driveway, there were no thank yous, no exchange of good wishes either, just Janet shouting that they'd see us in court.

* * *

The McDougalls left on a Wednesday. At six o'clock Sunday evening our next visitors arrived unexpectedly in a R.V. the size of a greyhound bus. Fortunately, they couldn't get it into our driveway. They parked the monster temporarily on the road.

It wasn't that we were unaware that Tony, Gordon's old school friend, and his new wife, Pam, were on their way from England and slated to drop in on us. We just expected them to let us know when the container ship they were travelling on docked in Quebec City - then, keep us posted about when they planned to arrive at our place.

Pam had telephoned frequently over the winter - between their trips to the Greek islands, Spain, Morocco, Portugal and the South Seas - updating their summer plans to tour eastern Canada and the U.S. I had the misfortune to pick up the telephone for most of these calls.

"We'll be along your way sometime after the middle of July," Pam informed me in early June, once their itinerary was finalized. "Our boat's supposed to sail on the fifteenth. Arrival in Quebec City depends on conditions at sea. We'll keep you posted."

Although I protested, as I had before, that this summer wasn't a good time for us, Pam, who arranged not only their itineraries but all aspects of her life and Tony's, told me in what seemed to me an overly cheery and irritatingly assertive nursing home voice, "Now then, Luv, not to worry, I understand how tired and a bit creaky old people get. Just give us a look in though. All Tony wants is to have a few beers and a chat with Gordon. For old times sake, you know. This might be the old boys' last chance for a get-together."

While acknowledging to myself that this might indeed be the case, I still found my antagonism to Pam's insistence growing.

Probably it's just that I haven't recovered from the McDougalls' visit, I rationalized. Nevertheless, I still resented being bamboozled.

While I tried to control my increasing hostility to this determined woman, Pam hastened on: "And by the way, we're not going to stop with you. We've booked a caravan in Quebec City, so we'll be self-sufficient."

It was obvious that Pam was used to getting her own way, and, that, having managed a nursing home for ten years prior to her marriage to Tony, she was a pro at bossing old people. Twenty-six years Tony and Gordon's junior - and twenty years mine - she was indeed a spring chicken by our reckoning. *An obnoxious spring chicken*, I told myself privately.

*　*　*

Despite Pam's organizational skills and the brand new cell phone resting handily between the two bucket seats in their lavishly-appointed R.V., neither she nor Tony managed a call to let us know their whereabouts - nothing from Quebec City, nothing from Matapédia, nothing even from Moncton, when they were almost on our doorstep.

Nevertheless, it was clear that they expected dinner. Although I wanted to say that we'd already eaten an hour earlier because we had had no warning of their imminent arrival, I couldn't bring myself to say so.

Instead, I suggested that Gordon take them to the nearest trailer park, book them in there and bring them back in our car for drinks. By then, I'd have their dinner under way.

Thank God for the freezer, I thought. Something for every eventuality there. Should it be seafood casserole or beef Stroganoff? I opted for the latter because I figured Tony and Pam had likely been abstaining from British beef on account of the continuing threat of mad cow disease.

While I peeled potatoes and the casserole defrosted, I also thanked the powers that be for the fact that their R.V. was too large to fit in our driveway. Our encroaching shrubs and overhanging boughs of pine and linden were the cause. Gordon cannot bring himself to cut them back.

*   *   *

When Pam had told me months ago that they were planning to rent a *caravan*, I couldn't help conjuring up in my mind's eye the gaudily-painted horse-drawn Gypsy conveyance depicted in a book I had read avidly as a ten-year-old. So, over before-dinner drinks in the deck chairs overlooking the lake, when, hoping to put everyone at ease, I laughingly told Pam and Tony that we'd half expected them to arrive in a horse-drawn Gypsy caravan, Pam was not amused.

"I'm not all that keen on animals," she told us. "Especially horses.... I'm very glad not to have lived back in the horse and buggy days. It's driving motor cars I've a passion for."

"Driving that HUGE R.V. must have been quite a challenge, though," I observed. "On the wrong side of the road and all," I quipped.

"Not at all," Pam countered. "We loved every moment of the trip. Didn't we, Tony?"

Tony nodded benignly. As far as I know, Tony has always been amiable - and uncontentious. It's hard to be absolutely sure though. I scarcely know him and hadn't seen him for over forty years. But I remember Gordon telling me that when he met Tony - on his first day at a new school - they had a fistfight in the bicycle shed, an incident which they say was the beginning of their friendship. They both seem quite proud of that scuffle.

I find this hard to fathom, but then people are always surprising me. That's partly why I find them so fascinating - for the most part.

I am also surprised that Gordon and Tony still keep in touch, after a fashion. Their lives have been so different, and neither one is much of a correspondent. Mostly, over the years, they tended to write at Christmas, but since Tony divorced his last wife four years ago and promptly married Pam, she has taken over this chore. She sends out a competent but uninspiring once-a-year form letter, which seems to suit Tony fine, but, understandably, exasperates Gordon no end. These letters mostly recount Tony and Pam's purchases and peregrinations. One year, because of their travels, their Christmas communiqué arrived at the beginning of October.

Tony has coasted through life: Gordon has had to work. Tony has never had to think about money because he was born with a silver spoon in his mouth: Gordon had to pull himself up by his bootstraps.

When they met, at the age of fourteen, neither Tony nor Gordon liked school. Gordon, however, had to persevere; Tony didn't. Since Tony's father died that year and Tony fell heir to a couple of factories and a fortune, dropping out of school right away seemed like a convenient option. No one objected.

While his mother and aunt ran the factories with the help of very competent and experienced upper management, already in place, Tony was groomed for his eventual takeover. Although his mother and aunt agreed that he would learn the business from the ground up, they didn't push him. While these middle-aged women slaved to make a success of their new responsibility, they spared Tony the struggle. Partly this was because they were having the time of their lives managing such a significant empire and proving their business competence; and partly it was that they both idolized Tony, their only family tie to the next generation. Preserving him, stress free, was every bit as important to their plans as making a success of managing the factories.

Since Pam was mostly controlling our conversation, Gordon and Tony hadn't had a chance to indulge in reminiscences of times past. Because these were all pre-Pam, I was pretty sure they weren't going to get back to discussing old times. So, I thought I'd ask about their trip over. Anyway, I was curious to know why, if they'd wanted to travel by sea, they hadn't come first class on a luxury liner.

With money no object, why, I wondered, choose a container ship? In my mind, container ships are associated with stowaways - the only newsworthy passengers I'd heard of travelling on these immense and, it seems to me, not-very-aesthetically-pleasing vessels.

While I was deciding how to pose the question diplomatically so as not to offend Pam, Gordon jumped in with the same question, apparently having no qualms about how to phrase it.

"So you two," Gordon began, "how's life aboard ship as stowaways? Tell us how it happened."

Tony laughed. Pam didn't. I thought nostalgically how differently Joyce, Tony's first wife, would have responded. Her jolly, throaty chuckle, developed early on, I guessed, while waiting on appreciative customers - Tony among them - in her father's pub, was contagious, lightening moods.

Tony was about to answer Gordon, but Pam beat him to it.

"Well, about how we got on this container ship... Tony had cargo on it - a considerable lot of stuff from one of the factories. And when, just by way of casual conversation, he asked the captain if he ever carried passengers, the captain said that actually he did from time to time. There was, he said, a very nice roomy outside cabin next to his own. Although it was reserved for the owners, they hardly ever used it... Why? he asked. Was Tony interested in a sea voyage?

"So when Tony came home and talked to me, we decided that would be just the ticket. We accepted the captain's offer, and that was that.

"And you should have seen the cabin. Huge. Gorgeous. And the meals we took with the captain! Absolutely gourmet! And what a marvelous choice of spirits and wines!"

"Wasn't it thoughtful of the captain to make you such a present?" I said, thinking that indeed the very rich get all the perks.

"Well, not exactly a present," Tony interrupted. "The passage cost £900 for each of us, each way. £3600 in all.... Still a bargain, though. Wined and dined us like royalty."

* * *

When I went inside to see how dinner was coming along, Gordon followed me. He needed to replenish the drinks.

"Pam seems quite nice and very devoted to Tony," he began, then added apologetically, "but she is a bit of a wet blanket, I find.... Not altogether her fault really. It's just that everything between Tony and me goes back long before Pam. I don't want to hurt her feelings by talking about that time. Also, I'm frightened to death of embarrassing them both by forgetting and bringing up Joyce and the children.

"By the way, how do you think Tony looks?" I asked as I opened the front door so that Gordon wouldn't have to put the drink tray down.

"Pretty bad. Didn't recognize him at all at first. Carrying all that weight so he can hardly walk.... Doesn't look as if he'll hold up much longer." Then as an afterthought, Gordon added, "But you have to give Pam credit for looking after him well. She guards his every move."

"So, is that the kind of care you'd like?" I couldn't help

saying. I don't know, though, whether, as the door came to behind him, Gordon heard me.

* * *

We ate outside in the deck chairs. The dining room table was piled high with my students' papers and essays. The
class had been a large one and I hadn't finished marking their
papers. I would have to stay up late: the marks were due on
Monday.

With this task looming, I excused myself after serving
coffee and liqueurs and went inside to work on the papers. Perhaps, I thought, the conversation will go better without me.

Before Gordon drove Tony and Pam back to the trailer
park, they breezed in to say good-bye to me. When I wished
them all the best on the rest of their trip, Pam cut me off. "Oh,
we're just off to Halifax for a couple of days. Not to worry, Luv,
we'll be back before you know we're gone. We'll all have more
time together then."

* * *

Next day, after turning in my marks just before the Ex-
tension Department office closed, I heaved a sigh of relief as I
turned the car homeward. Just the two of us, I thought. We'll
have the seafood casserole and scalloped potatoes - after a swim
and a glass of wine. Just ourselves. No visitors. Wonderful!

But I was mistaken. When I turned into our driveway
two cars with American plates were parked close to the house.
Their owners, I found, as soon as I stepped inside, were well
ensconced - one couple on the living room couch, the other in
the two most comfortable chairs.

But who were these four old people anyway? I had absolutely no idea. My face must have registered my incomprehension because Gordon, both women and one of the men started talking at once - all apparently eager to enlighten me. When they paused, I was no wiser.

Gordon took over. He was brief and to the point. "These two couples have just come from a conference in Halifax, which is where they met and, when they were chatting, they realized they both had a Maritime connection - us. Well, the connection is to you actually."

Still none the wiser, I said, "Oh," and waited for the rest of the explanation.

Turning first to the couple on the couch, Gordon announced, "This is your cousin Julian - well, second cousin, I guess, is more correct - and his wife, Judith, from Berkeley."

I nodded and mumbled something like, "I'm sorry for seeming so dense, but I didn't know I had a cousin Julian."

"Well, I didn't know about you either, until recently," the tall, stooped and emaciated man replied, in an agreeable, though somewhat ingratiating and tremulous voice. "You see, in my spare time I'm into genealogy. Something of a change, you know, from my genetics research at the university. It was through my genealogical connections I discovered you - and since Judith and I were already coming to this Halifax conference, looking you up seemed like a good idea."

"Oh I see," I replied, thinking I'd like to say that looking us up and appearing out of the blue like this was *not* a good idea at all.

"And," Gordon proceeded to explain, when he realized I was unlikely to say anything more just then to my new-found cousin and his wife, "these are Dr. and Mrs. Ernest Tremont - also from the U.S., from Chicago. Mrs. Tremont was briefly a student staying in the same residence as you in Saskatoon..., and Dr. Tremont, who was also at the U. of S., says he met you there once."

While I was racking my brains and thinking that neither of the Tremonts looked like anyone I'd ever seen before, Mrs. Tremont interrupted Gordon in a booming voice. "Elizabeth?... Or do you go by Liz or Beth?... "You look like you don't remember me, but I guess that's understandable. We didn't hang around together, didn't move with the same crowd. The reason I remember you is because at the frosh week dance you were chosen campus queen... or first princess... I don't remember which. My Ernie, here, was one of the judges, which is how he got to meet you."

"Umm," I said, wondering what you say to someone who claims acquaintance, yet is unsure of your given name. I changed the subject and asked, "How did you find our address? That must have taken considerable sleuthing."

"Not really," Jackie explained. "The *Alumni News*. There was something about you in there a while back. Something about a book or books, I think. Started off saying you lived in the Maritimes... I meant to go back and read the piece through, but you know how it is... The phone rings and you get sidetracked... The paper gets thrown out... But I did remember about you being in the Maritimes, so when Ernie said we were going to this conference in Halifax, all I had to do was e-mail the Alumni Office to get your address."

"Oh, I see," was all I said at first; then added, "It is too bad, though, you didn't let us know you were coming. If you had, I could have given you something to eat. As it is, I only have supper for the two of us."

"And what were you going to have then?" Judith inquired with some considerable interest. "Seafood, I'll bet?"

Perhaps if I hadn't been so exhausted I might have defended myself better, have suggested that we were just going to have eggs and toast - and that we had only three eggs left. But since prevarication is not my long suit even when I'm well rested and have my wits about me, I came out with the truth. "Well, yes, seafood casserole and scalloped potatoes."

"Seafood casserole and scalloped potatoes!" three of the four interlopers chorused.

"Sounds absolutely divine," Judith purred. "Couldn't you just add a few more ingredients? And by the way, what ingredients did you use?" she probed.

Foolishly again, I admitted not only to having made the dish with scallops and lobster, but to having more of the same in the freezer.

"Oh, then we're all set, aren't we?" Judith persisted. "My mouth's watering already. We don't mind waiting. The extra time will give us a chance to get acquainted."

* * *

Before I went out to the kitchen, I knew I had to pull myself together enough to ask our visitors where they had booked rooms for the night.

"Oh, we haven't made reservations," Jackie said. "We thought we'd just play things by ear. Be spontaneous, you know. We've had to think ahead all these years: it's great now to be able *to go with the flow*, as the kids say."

Seeing right away the direction this line of reasoning was taking, Gordon jumped in. Clearing his throat, the way he does when he is about to make an announcement he'd prefer not to, he said, "Well, I think we'd better find you a place to stay. Accommodations around here are almost impossible to book on the spur of the moment this time of year..."

"I'm afraid we can't put you up here because we're starting out for our island place at three in the morning.... We have to leave then so we'll be in time for the ferry. It crosses at six.

Tonight Elizabeth has to get our supplies organized carefully because there are no stores on the island. These preparations take some time."

A considerable pause ensued while our audience struggled to take in this information. Then my 'cousin' spoke up. "Well now, that sounds really intriguing. Why don't we all go along? Make an expedition of it...."

Judith clapped her hands in the manner of the coy three-year-old she must once have been. She was clearly about to enthuse when Gordon cleared his throat again. He had obviously learned from the last two invasions that one of us was going to have to think and act quickly and decisively if we weren't going to go under.

"I'm afraid that won't be possible." Gordon was blunt. His lips were tightly drawn against his teeth, a mannerism he has when he is seething. "We have no extra room over there.... Only one bedroom, no power, no running water.... Oh, and an outdoor privy."

Thank God! I thought as I watched these facts slowly registering. It appeared that Gordon had actually discouraged these intruders.

Judith, though, was quick to spot a possible loophole. "Well, that's too bad. Still, everything will work out fine. We can stay here; do you the favor of house sitting while you're away."

Gordon didn't miss a beat. With obviously heightened visions of these people staying on and taking over - shades of Josh and Janet - he announced firmly, "That will not be possible. We shut off the pump when we go away. That means there's no water."

Although it is the truth that we always take this precaution when we leave the house for more than a day, I wouldn't have had the presence of mind just then to have remembered to say so. Gordon stood up and looked around the room, like an old lion cornered and about to spring. He had had enough. And when Gordon is really fed up there's no mistaking his mood. Another out-of-place comment from one of these people and he was going to lose his temper. When that happens fireworks ensue. Insensitive as these visitors seemed, they suddenly appeared to decide as one that tangling with Gordon was a bad idea.

After a lot of futile telephone calls, our defeated foursome found rooms - but not nearby. Since they had to drive to Saint John, they left our place while it was still light.

*   *   *

Gordon and I did indeed make our getaway shortly after three the next morning. We'd had only a couple of hours sleep, certainly not enough for a couple of oldsters. It had taken until after midnight to get our gear and provisions together. Still we weren't tempted to stick around and rest up. It was anyone's guess who would turn up next. Escaping prisoners couldn't have been more focused on getting away quickly.

At first, though, our flight didn't bring the kind of hoped-for relief. We were so exhausted that we could hardly manage the dark drive along the Sunrise Trail and the wait for the 'ferry' - a thirty-five foot Cape Islander - which takes foot passengers back and forth to the island four days a week.

*   *   *

Jeff, the owner and captain of the *Moonshiner*, welcomed us aboard enthusiastically, stowed our gear and provisions with his usual good humor and efficiency, and retired to the cabin. Since it was almost time to leave, it seemed as if we were to be the only passengers on this run.

Gordon and I settled into two of the white plastic chairs in the stern. Outside was the place to be on such a clear, calm morning.

Above us on the wharf an old man with a rod and a bucket beside him was fishing for mackerel. Below, and off to the side, gulls, terns and cormorants boated at ease, as unruffled as plastic ducks in a bathtub. On the breakwater at the harbor entrance battalions of sea birds were perched strategically on nearly every rock watching intently for schools of fish entering or leaving the harbor.

After coming outside once more to scan the wharf for latecomers and spotting none, Jeff returned to the cabin and started the motor. He eased the *Moonshiner* past *Strait Lady*, *Breakwater Dancer*, and *Kate and Mary*, boats which had served well in lobster season and were tied up and idle until their owners decided whether or not it was worth their while to go for herring when that season opened.

Soothed by the warming sun, the salt smell, and the steady throb of the motor, Gordon and I fell asleep. Forty minutes later, when the motor stopped, we woke to see a throng of islanders - well, a throng by island standards, which translates as about fifteen people - looking down at us, smiling ... ready to help us up the ladder, unload our gear, give us a lift to our place ... whatever it took. We were their people. They were ours. And I thought, as old friends hugged us and said they'd been worried about our absence, this is where we should stay.

ABOUT THE AUTHOR

Allison Mitcham is the author of a number of successful books. Several have been on best-seller lists. In 1994 she received British Columbia's Lieutenant Governor's award for *Taku*. Mitcham is professor emeritus of English at the Université de Moncton where she taught graduate and undergraduate literature courses for twenty years before retiring and devoting herself exclusively to writing. She has published 28 books in the past 30 years, as well as scores of poems and articles.